PUFFIN BOOKS

# MAX
## KOWALSKI
### DIDN'T MEAN IT

D0299902

# MAX
## KOWALSKI
## DIDN'T MEAN IT

SUSIE DAY

**PUFFIN**

PUFFIN BOOKS

UK | USA | Canada | Ireland | Australia
India | New Zealand | South Africa

Puffin Books is part of the Penguin Random House group of companies
whose addresses can be found at global.penguinrandomhouse.com.

www.penguin.co.uk
www.puffin.co.uk
www.ladybird.co.uk

First published 2019

001

Text copyright © Susie Day, 2019
Cover artwork © Andrew Bannecker, 2019

Set in 11.75/16 pt Baskerville MT Std
Typeset by Jouve (UK), Milton Keynes
Printed and bound in Great Britain by Clays Ltd, Elcograf S.p.A.

A CIP catalogue record for this book is available from the British Library

ISBN: 978-0-241-35139-0

All correspondence to:
Puffin Books
Penguin Random House Children's
80 Strand, London WC2R ORL

*To Jenny, who has the best ideas*

There are times in life when everything stands still, like God pressed pause.

As if you know you'll remember it forever.

As if you can go back.

Max would never forget standing on the mountain, holding the knife. A bitter wind blowing through his coat. Snow on the rocks. Jagged grey spikes of stone poking up out of the ground like a long spine, like wings, like a vicious tail . . .

Except they were just rocks. And Max said to himself: *Max, you muppet, there's no such thing as dragons.*

Then he heard the roaring, and the rocks began to move.

I

'It's not my fault, Mr Brew,' said Max.

'It never is,' sighed Mr Brew. 'Go on. What is it this time? Did it sprout wings and fly away? Or perhaps you got amnesia, and forgot you had any homework?'

That wasn't fair. As if he'd pretend to have amnesia more than once, to the same teacher.

And it really wasn't his fault, this time.

Monday mornings were never Max's best. This one had started with Ripley waking him up by sitting on his chest, pressing her face close to his, and whispering with hot breath, 'There's something gone wrong with my earthworm,' before opening her sticky hand right under his nose.

There *was* something gone wrong with her earthworm. It was dead. Stiff and curled, like a salt-and-vinegar French Fry. Which was what happened when you put an earthworm in your hoodie pocket for a week and forgot about it.

He'd told her it was no use as a pet.

Loads of times.

But Ripley was six, and people who are six never listen to anyone, apparently.

'Geroff,' said Max, pushing her off his bunk on to the floor. Like anyone would.

Ripley hit the floor with a thud and yelled like she was being murderized.

That woke up Thelma and Louise, the twins, who were nine and never listened to him either.

'What? What's going on? Help! Fire! *Aaaargh!*' yelled Thelma from the other top bunk, scrabbling for her glasses.

'That's not very helpful,' said Louise quietly from her bottom bunk.

'Look what Max did!' wailed Ripley, thrusting the stiff, curled and now snapped-in-half earthworm at Thelma.

'Max! You killed it!'

'I did not!'

'It's pretty bloody dead!'

'Well, I didn't kill it!'

'Oi!' came a deep yell from the front room. 'Somebody's trying to sleep in here, remember?'

They all hushed at once. Their dad, Big Pete Kowalski, did shifts driving a forklift in a warehouse. Four nights a week, he was a bouncer on the doors at Voodoo nightclub. If he wasn't on a job, his mornings were for sleeping.

'But my worm . . .' mumbled Ripley.

Thelma glared at Max from her top bunk from behind her pink-rimmed glasses.

He was never going to get any peace now.

'Come on,' he said.

They all tiptoed to the kitchen, Max and Ripley and the twins. Ripley laid the two curled ends forlornly on the table.

'Worms can regrow themselves,' said Louise, tucking her long pale hair behind one ear before leaning in for a closer look. 'If you chop one in half, it grows itself a new bottom.'

'That's disgusting,' said Thelma.

'It's not! Annelids are amazing. Did you know –?'

'Didn't know, don't care,' said Thelma.

'Can it grow a new bottom even after it's dead?' asked Ripley.

They all looked at the crispy worm-halves.

Louise looked at Max, a concerned crinkle in the centre of her forehead.

'I reckon not,' said Max, in a soft voice.

So instead of going back to bed, Max had to hold an earthworm funeral – which meant sneaking out of the flat to Mrs Gupta's three doors down in the freezing cold to bury it in the hard earth of her yucca plant, and everyone having to say a little something about how much the earthworm had meant to them, what a shining light it had been in their lives, how it had gone to a better place, and so on.

5

'You will always be remembered as . . . a worm that lived in my pocket,' said Ripley solemnly.

Thelma laughed.

Max kicked her.

Thelma kicked him back.

Then Ripley burst into tears, and Max had to carry her indoors and shove her under a duvet to muffle all the sobbing.

Dad always said that was the trouble with girls: they kept all their feelings on their outsides. Being a boy was a lot less drama.


Mondays were always a bit of a scramble to get everyone out of the house. Max had to find his Sunbrook Academy uniform that he'd put somewhere on Friday, and that was ages ago. He had to get all the knots out of Ripley's blonde curls, and tie them up in bunches, and make sure she'd done a wee. He had to drag Thelma out of the bathroom, where she would be fussing with her hair (short and choppy, as unlike Louise's bum-length ponytail as possible). He had to distract Louise from whatever book her nose was pressed into. And all that in time to walk the three of them to Pilton Road Primary and then get to Sunbrook only ten minutes late. With all the worm business on top, there was definitely no time for breakfast.

And that meant he didn't see the nearly empty box of Krispies, which meant he forgot to turn it into a 3D model of Southend Pier for his Design and Technology Structures from Around the World homework. In fact, he didn't even know he'd forgotten until he walked into Miss Clay's classroom.

Judah had made the Sydney Opera House out of paper plates.

Ismael had built a Lego Disneyland, with a rollercoaster and a pirate ship.

Elis Evans had made the Golden Gate Bridge out of clay, straws and thread, and mounted it on a long plank of wood.

Elis Evans was Max's best friend.

He looked at Max's empty hands.

'You could say we did it together,' Elis Evans said quietly. 'I wouldn't mind.'

Max looked at the Golden Gate Bridge. It was really good. It was solidly built, with two strong clay towers, a fretwork of straw struts underneath, and impossibly delicate threads sewn into loops to show the engineering. It was painted a deep reddish brown, and dotted with tiny clay cars painted silver, blue and yellow. There was even a real river flowing underneath at the front: a foil tray on the wooden plank, filled up from a water bottle. It must have taken Elis Evans ages, even with his mum's help. It must have taken him all weekend.

No one would believe Max had anything to do with it.

'S'fine,' said Max.

Which was why he'd only been at school for fifteen minutes and was now standing in front of Mr Brew, Deputy Head, in trouble, again.

Mr Brew tapped his pen on his desk, waiting.

'So, sir, what happened was, I had to hold an earthworm funeral,' said Max.

It turned out that telling the truth wasn't any different from telling Mr Brew you'd been kidnapped, or abducted by aliens.

Max spent morning break and half of lunch sitting in the Reflection Room.

'Oh dear, Max, I was hoping I might not see you *quite* so soon this week,' said Mrs Carty, who supervised most days. 'No packed lunch? I can bring you in a tray from the hall, lovey.'

Max shook his head. Mrs Carty would bring him slippery pasta twirls in slippery pasta sauce, and stand over him until he'd eaten it all. Hungry was better.

Mr Brew decided he'd done enough Reflecting with ten minutes of lunch break left.

Elis Evans was having a music lesson, so Max went to play football on the field with the lads.

It was boring. No one would kick to him. It was the end of November and he didn't have a coat, and it was freezing if you weren't running around. Max went back inside, to the Design and Technology block, and stared at all the Structures from Around the World projects lined up on the side in Miss Clay's class.

Amber had made the Eiffel Tower out of a million lolly sticks.

Olivia Button had done the London Eye with a bike wheel that really turned.

Max thought maybe it wasn't so bad that he'd forgotten to make Southend Pier out of an empty Krispies box.

He leaned over Ismael's Lego Disneyland.

Elis Evans had all the pirate Lego at his house. Max's mum used to take him round there to play with it after school. Elis Evans's mum and Max's mum would drink a hundred cups of tea and say, 'Oh, I shouldn't,' every time they ate a biscuit. Elis Evans would build a treasure island, and move all the pirates into houses. And Max would get cannons and explode everything into bits.

It seemed like a long time ago now.

Max poked the pirate ship, to see if it swung.

A bit of the Lego came off, where it wasn't quite stuck down.

Max tried to put it back, but his hand knocked over one of the palm trees.

'What are you doing, Max Kowalski?'

It was Amber, her face pinched and pink.

'Nothing,' said Max, straightening up.

Judah and Ismael were close behind, sweaty from football.

'What's he doing?' asked Ismael.

'He's messing with your Disneyland, Ismael,' said Amber.

'No I'm not,' said Max, reaching out one finger and tipping over another palm tree. Just because.

'Don't you dare,' said Ismael, stepping forward and rolling up his sleeves.

'Or what?' said Max, knocking the car off the top of the rollercoaster.

Judah pushed forward and grabbed Max's shirt in his fist. 'Knock it off,' Judah said.

Max hated being held on to if he hadn't said he wanted to be held on to. He pulled away – and Judah held on tighter – and Max raised his fist – and Judah raised his as well and began to swing, too slow and lumbering and obvious for Max to let him anywhere near a target.

Max ducked. Then he pulled his arm right back, ready to thump Judah really hard in his big meaty mouth . . . except, instead, his elbow connected sharply with something behind him.

There was an almighty clattering crash.

When Max turned round, Elis Evans's Golden Gate Bridge was in many, many fractured red-brown pieces on the floor.

# 2

Max was sent back to the Reflection Room for the rest of the day.

Mrs Carty gave him a worksheet about the pyramids.

Max tipped back in his chair the way she didn't like, and Reflected that the weird stain on the ceiling where a pipe was leaking looked like a dog; and that if he could order a pizza right now, he would get one with extra cheese and pepperoni and sweetcorn and NO MUSHROOMS and not have to share it with anyone; and that he wanted to go round Elis Evans's house and build him a massive island with his pirate Lego, really, really carefully, to show he was sorry.

At home time, Mr Brew came to sit with him while they waited for Dad to come in for A Talk. Mr Brew looked as if it was his Golden Gate Bridge that Max had smashed to bits all over the floor: all sighs and sloping shoulders.

'You know we all care about you here, Max, don't you? Everyone at this school. We know you've had a rough run of it. We're all sympathetic to your . . . situation.'

The 'situation' was Max's mum, who had been knocked down by a car and killed, instantly they said, two years ago. No one ever said her name, though. No one ever said 'mum'.

He missed hearing it.

Mr Brew lifted his arm, as if he wanted to put his arm round Max, then awkwardly tapped his shoulder instead.

Max shut his eyes. It was *his* mum that wasn't here any more, not Mr Brew's. His being sad about it didn't make Max feel better.

Mr Brew sighed. 'I know there's a good kid in there, Max. He might be buried deep down out of sight, but he's there. A good, kind, bright young man. I see glimpses of him every day, I really do.'

Max thought there might not be a good kid in there, to be honest. Max thought he was a bit like an earthworm. He'd been chopped in half one day, and what grew back was all bad.

'But – we can't keep on like this, can we, hmm? Something has to change.'

'Yes, sir,' said Max, like always.

Then Dad arrived, and at once everything was all right.

Max could see him coming down the corridor, sweeping a path through the end-of-day hustle like a tidal wave, with a wink for Mrs Carty and a fist bump for a passing Year Ten. Big Pete Kowalski was six foot three and earned his name all over. Not fat exactly, just broad:

great thick arms, a round belly, and a back that could carry the world. Max was skinny, but Dad said that was normal for the men in their family at his age. Max was going to shoot up one of these days. Max was going to grow up to be six foot three too. Every day his dad wore biker boots and blue jeans, a plain white T-shirt and a leather jacket. Max wasn't dead set on the leather jacket, because Elis Evans said it was cruelty to animals. But he'd have the rest, when he was big. He'd have it all.

Big Pete Kowalski shook Mr Brew's hand, and sat in a too-low, too-small chair, his face open and smiling.

'Boys will be boys, eh?' he said. 'Bit of fisticuffs, bit of messing about. I was just the same, Mr Brew. He's like looking in a mirror, this one. My chip off the old block.'

Dad gave Max a gentle cuff round the back of his head, and Max felt warm and right and whole again.

Mr Brew straightened his shoulders.

'Mr Kowalski. Everyone here at Sunbrook respects the challenges you've faced. We all appreciate how difficult it can be . . . How much you care about your family.'

That was true. Everyone said so. He's a good dad, Big Pete, they said. He'd do anything for those kids. Four of them, and him all by himself, and he never asks for help.

Dad said it too. Ripley was his princess; the twins were his angels; Max was his big man. He said so all the time.

Mr Brew wasn't finished.

'But we can't ignore it when things go wrong, Mr Kowalski. Max's violent behaviour led to the complete destruction of another student's project.'

Dad looked at Max, waiting.

'I'm really sorry,' said Max quietly, because he was; his insides were all coiled up with it.

Dad lifted an eyebrow. Then he smiled.

'There you go, Mr Brew,' said Dad, slapping his knees firmly. 'The boy's sorry. No harm done. No bones broken. Come on, Max, let's go pick up those girls.'


When they all got home, the front room was full of boxes.

Cardboard boxes. Big ones, in stacks.

'Just looking after a few things for Nice Jackie,' said Dad. 'Won't be for long.'

Nice Jackie was Dad's boss at the club. She ran the funfair too, and she wore perfume that smelled like sweets. She had pretty yellow hair, and she always looked dressed up, like her life was a party. Once, Max had been with Dad when he dropped into her office at the club, and she'd ordered Max a Coke with ice and lemon and a straw. Everyone called her Nice Jackie, and that was why.

'I hope they put the heaviest boxes at the bottom,' said Louise, pulling her ponytail tighter. 'Though to be honest, a pyramid would've been much more structurally sound.'

'Who cares! What's inside?' asked Thelma, standing on tiptoes.

'Rabbits,' said Dad, flipping open the top of the nearest box.

Ripley's blue eyes went wide with hope. '*Real* rabbits?'

But the one he pulled out was fluffy pink and yellow, the kind you win at the fair, with blue glass eyes and plastic whiskers.

Ripley's face fell.

Max wouldn't have minded a real rabbit either. It had to be better than an earthworm.

The next day, Max took a tube of superglue to school.

'For the Golden Gate Bridge. To stick it back together,' he said, sitting down beside Elis Evans as usual.

Elis Evans shook his head. 'Me and Miss Clay thought about it, but there were just too many pieces. So it all got swept up and put in the big bins round the back.'

Max held the superglue tightly, squeezing it with his thumb so all the glue bulged at one end.

'Ripley wants a rabbit,' he said.

Elis Evans nodded. 'Nice. You should get one, then. They can be a bit mardy, though, rabbits. Especially the girl ones.'

'It'll fit in just fine at my house, then.'

Elis Evans snorted.

That was the good thing about having a best friend, Max thought. You could make a mistake, and the next day everything would be back to normal.

The superglue tube burst open at the seams and splattered all over the table.

Max put his hand in it, just to see what would happen.

They had to carry the table with him into the Reflection Room, and Mrs Carty spent all of morning break soaking it with stinky nail polish remover and warm water. Max's hand came away pink and stiff-skinned, as if it belonged to someone else.

When Max got home there were more boxes, built round the kitchen cupboards like a fence.

The next day there were even more, piled in the only empty space in the bedroom, between the two sets of bunk beds.

'Not cool, Papa,' said Thelma, squeezing herself awkwardly through the gap on their side.

'I think they might be a fire hazard,' said Louise.

'You're a fire hazard,' said Thelma.

'Rabbits,' sighed Ripley.

Max didn't mind. He quite liked having a wall between the bunk beds. It was almost like having his own room all to himself. He'd had one once, before the girls, before everything. There'd been just three of them then; there were photos to prove it. A house with a green garden, and little Max smiling on top of Dad's shoulders. His mum, her dark hair spilling forward as she bent to light two birthday candles on a football cake. But when he tried to remember, he could only see what was in the photos. The rest was lost.

'It's just for a couple more days,' Dad promised.

It was true. On Friday, Max was woken up in the middle of the night by Nice Jackie's boys, big lads in black, carrying the boxes out of the bedroom. He stayed stiff and still in bed till he could hear their boots thudding down the corridor outside, then he slid down from his bunk to peer out of the window. There was a van parked up on the pavement down below; Max could see his dad standing beside it in his leather jacket, under a street light.

Everyone else was asleep.

Max hesitated, just for a moment. Then he climbed up his bunk-bed ladder and flipped open the nearest cardboard box to get Ripley a rabbit. Nice Jackie wouldn't mind just one.

There weren't rabbits in this box, though. There were lots of big bottles of Smurnov vodka. In the next box there were Marylebone cigarettes.

Nice Jackie's boys came back while he still had his nose in a box.

'Back to bed, Max,' said one, quiet but firm.

So Nice Jackie's boys knew his name. It was a strangely nervous feeling. But he climbed back into bed anyway, rabbit-less, and made such convincing snoozing noises that he fell right back to sleep.

*

Usually Saturday mornings in the Kowalski house were no good. Dad, who didn't get home before four a.m., would be asleep in the front room, where the kitchen was and the big TV and the one comfy armchair they all fought over. Max, the twins and Ripley would have to stay in their room, where the little TV couldn't go above volume number six and there was always a fight over what to watch. Thelma was a hair-puller, and had learned a pretty savage arm-twist. But Max was bigger, and stronger, and all he had to do was sit on her till her breath ran out to win. Then he'd say, 'Who's the oldest?' and Ripley would squeak, 'You're the oldest!' Then Thelma would hand over the remote, and Max would put on whatever she didn't want to watch most, and Louise would look up from her book in her bunk-bed cave and frown.

It wasn't his fault he was the oldest.

But this Saturday, Dad was up and about and frying up bacon butties with loads of brown sauce on four of them, and no sauce for Max. He had to wake Max to eat his.

'Is it your birthday?' asked Ripley, licking his fingers.

'Nope,' said Dad. 'But we are celebrating, princess.'

Dad was all smiles as he slurped his tea on the sofa where he slept, his duvet and pillows already tidied away. He thumped a thick roll of notes on the coffee table, wrapped up in an elastic band. All twenties.

'Hell-o, Papa,' said Thelma, joining him on the sofa and wrapping her arms round his middle. 'You know I love you best, right?'

'Nice Jackie paid you all that money, just for rabbits?' asked Louise.

'Yep. Rabbits – very in demand these days, it turns out.'

Dad looked at Max as he said it and gave him a wink. He knew Max had seen what was in the other boxes, and he didn't mind. It was as if they had a secret to share, just between them.

Max grinned back. It was good being the oldest, sometimes.

Dad peeled twenties off the roll and gave them one each.

Ripley held hers close to her face, then rubbed it on her cheek.

'I'm going to buy a rabbit hutch,' she whispered.

'Bubblegum. And pens,' said Thelma. 'Pens with llamas on.'

Max rolled his eyes. Of course they'd have llamas on. All the girls at school had llama pencil cases and llama water-bottles and llama keyrings.

'Books,' said Louise. 'The new Dragonslayer Chronicles came out last week.'

Max rolled his eyes again. Louise didn't care about llamas; she loved a series about a girl called Kriss who wore armour and swords and fought dragons. She already had a stack of the books under her bed, the pages gone soft with rereading.

'I'm going to save mine up,' said Max, pressing his into the table so it would go flat.

There were trainers in the window of Denny's Sporting Goods: white Nikes, knocked down to fifty-five pounds. He wanted them. He needed them. He stopped to look at them every time they passed, to make sure they were still there, and now he was twenty quid closer to having them.

Ripley squashed her lips together.

'I'm going to save mine up too,' she said, with a sigh, and pressed hers against the table as well.

Dad raised his eyebrows. 'Oh-ho. Well then, I guess the treats are on me today, eh? Day at the beach . . . what do you say?'

They all grinned then, because Southend beach was the best and so was their dad when he took them.

It wasn't like going in summer, Max thought: gritty sand between his toes, sticky sun-cream on his skin; bodies and noises, in a tight press all around. It was the second of December now. There were star-shaped lights on every lamp post, and the beach was cold and quiet and mostly empty: one chippy, one cafe, one hopeful stallholder selling buckets and spades, tied down with tape to stop the wind stealing them away across the sand.

That was how Max liked it. Like it was theirs.

They had hot chips, and candyfloss, and a go on the train down Southend Pier (even though they'd all been on it a hundred times) just to be in the warm. Then they went round all the games in the funfair: Bash the Rat and

Flip the Frog. Max had to lift Ripley up so she could reach. Every other time she'd ended up in tears of frustration, but this time Dad spent eighteen quid so she could keep going till that rubber frog finally landed on a lily pad.

'You've won a prize, darling!' said the man behind the counter. 'What do you want?'

There were lollies and a magic set and a fluffy tiger that was obviously the best thing there. But Ripley wasn't having any advice off Max.

'*That* one,' she said firmly, pointing a finger.

The man tugged a pink and yellow rabbit with blue glass eyes off the rack and pressed it into her arms.

'They're very in demand these days,' said Ripley darkly, and she skipped away hugging it.

Max went on Shoot the Tins, three shots for a pound.

His first shot missed by a mile.

Max felt stiff all over. He wanted to be good at this. He was meant to be good at this. When he watched movies with his dad, the heroes were always picking up guns and hitting the target dead on. If he was in a movie, Max would definitely be the hero. So shooting stuff? Yeah, Max Kowalski can do that.

Dad took the gun from him with a grunt and leaned down to take the second shot, lining up the sights.

That missed by a mile too.

The girl behind the counter twisted her lips into a sour smile.

'Harder than it looks, eh, big man?'

Max bunched a fist, because no one talked to Big Pete Kowalski like that.

But then his dad leaned in close behind him, his warm leather-jacket smell enveloping Max, his broad shoulders strong behind Max's back, and he slipped the gun back into Max's hands.

'It's rigged, kiddo. Do it just like you did before – but don't aim at the tin. Aim to the left. Just to the left.'

Max listened. Max fired.

*Ping!* went the tin.

'Well done,' said the sour girl, not warmly. 'Choose your prize, love.'

There were lollies and a magic set and a fluffy tiger here too. But Dad shook his head, throwing the gun down on the counter with a clatter.

'You can keep your prize.'

'Keep your prize,' echoed Max, feeling proud as Dad stalked away.

He didn't want that tiger anyway.

They left the fair after that.

They went to Fallowfield shops, for bubblegum and llama pens and the new Dragonslayer Chronicles.

'I'm going to name my rabbit after my favourite most loved best thing,' Ripley announced as they walked home.

'Hey!' said Dad. 'You can't call it Daddy, princess. It'll get confused.'

Ripley stuck out her tongue. 'Duh!' she said, poking his elbow. 'This rabbit is called . . . Potatoes.'

'You can't call a rabbit Potatoes either,' said Louise, not looking up, her nose already in her book. 'There's only one of it.'

'Pota*to*, then. And I can, too. Because I love my rabbit, and I love potatoes. Chips and crisps and mashed potato . . .'

'Potato waffles,' said Thelma. 'And curly fries.'

'Roasties,' murmured Louise.

'Potato salad,' said Dad.

'Just potatoes,' said Max. 'You know. Boiled. With butter on.'

It turned out potatoes were one thing they could all agree on.

When Max climbed into bed, Ripley was still half awake, hugging Potato with both arms and both legs like she was trying to climb a rope.

'Max?' she said sleepily. 'If you had a rabbit to name, and you named it after your favourite most loved best thing, what would it be called?'

Max thought about the Nike trainers in the window – but he didn't have them yet. He thought about the week when Sunbrook Academy flooded and he got three days off, not going to school at all. Then he thought about the twenty-pound note, and the fair, and Dad giving him a wink, just between them.

'Today,' he said. That's what he'd call it, because not every day was as good as this one.

# 3

On Sunday, Max went round to Elis Evans's house.

Number 17 Carmody Avenue was at the top of town, with views across the sea. You could see Southend Pier when you were having a wee at Elis Evans's house. You had to take your shoes off in the porch, and they had the sort of fridge that poured ice-cold water out of a tap in the door, and a biscuit tin that was always full.

'Max,' said Elis Evans's mum when she opened the door. 'I'll say it now: you aren't going to break anything today. Not a question, more of a statement. All right? Agreed? Good.'

Elis Evans's mum had been best friends with Max's mum before she died, which was why Max had been coming round to play with Elis Evans's pirate Lego for years.

She was soft-bodied, and she smelled of rose petals and cups of tea, all things Mum-like. Max missed his mum, missed her always, but he kept it apart from himself, like a balloon tied on a string. It bobbed above his head but it did not touch him, and he did not touch it. Except sometimes, when Mrs Evans made him dinner and remembered to make sure none of the beans on his plate touched his toast.

She was a puzzle. But he did like the biscuit tin.

'I'll be good, Mrs Evans,' said Max, toeing off his not-white, not-Nike, not-fifty-five-pound trainers and putting them carefully by the door. 'Promise.'

'Good,' said Elis Evans's mum. Then her face went soft and sad. 'So like her, you are. She never told the truth neither.' She reached out to ruffle his hair fondly. Max leaned ever so slightly backwards.

Elis Evans's mum sighed. 'Go on up, then. He's in his room.'

Max escaped as quickly as he could.

Elis Evans had a huge room all to himself on the first floor of the house. It was usually a cheerful mess of whatever he was into at the time: lemons generating enough electricity to power a light bulb; remote-control cars; volcanoes. But today the carpet had been rolled back to show bare paint-speckled floorboards, and all his games and books were piled on the landing.

Elis Evans was sitting up one of two ladders in the middle of the room, looking at the ceiling.

'Mum says she's going to redecorate my bedroom in time for the Christmas holidays,' he said. 'She says it can be any colour I want except black, because if we ever sold the house we'd have to redecorate or they'd think we were Satanists. I thought kingfisher blue, because I'm going to take up birdwatching. I'm getting binoculars for Christmas. The only trouble is: what if after Christmas I get into space travel, or archaeology, instead? I suppose it would be hard to paint it the colour of archaeology, though. And kingfisher blue is just blue, really. Not that we are selling the house. My nain's selling hers, though – you know, my granny. In north Wales your granny is called your nain. We go and stay with her on holiday every summer and go up Snowdon mountain. Her house is called Tŷ Gwyn, which means "White House" in Welsh. If we painted this house all blue, we could call it Tŷ Glas, although I don't know the word for kingfisher; that's just ordinary blue. And we're not in Wales, so people would get confused. Anyway, my nain says she's too old to go up mountains now, so she lives in a home and she's trying to sell her house and we'll have to go somewhere else on holiday next summer. I want to go to Mexico. Or Iceland to see puffins. Or to the jazz festivals in New Orleans.'

'Sweet,' said Max.

Elis Evans was the quiet one at school, but at home he talked and talked. Max found it peaceful.

Max climbed up the other ladder to look at the ceiling too. Then Elis Evans fetched some string and a small yellow plastic bucket, the kind for sandcastles. He rigged up a pulley system between the ladders, and they spent all afternoon transporting secret spy messages and wounded

Lego people and egg sandwiches between them, until Max decided, just out of curiosity, to see if it would transport him too.

It wouldn't.

The string snapped. Max ended up on the floor with a crash – followed by one of the ladders.

'I didn't mean it,' said Max, as he limped into the porch.

'I know, Max,' said Elis Evans's mum in a tired voice. 'You never do.'

When Max got home, there were boxes in the front room again.

'More rabbits,' whispered Ripley, her arm wrapped tightly round Potato's neck.

'More twenty-pound notes,' said Thelma, meaning-fully.

No one complained this time, when all week more boxes arrived to fill up the front room and the gap between the bunk beds.

Max didn't look inside this time, either.

Nice Jackie's boys came round late on Friday night to take them away. Max kept his eyes shut tight, like in the deepest sleep, till they were gone.

He dreamed of glowing white trainers in Elis Evans's mum's porch.

But this Saturday morning, there were no bacon butties.

There were no twenty-pound notes.

There was no Dad sleeping on the sofa, either. His duvet and pillows were all folded away.

'He must have gone out to buy bacon,' suggested Louise, looking at the empty hook where he always hung his leather jacket.

'Or brown sauce,' said Thelma. 'Because *someone* finished the bottle last time.'

'I did not!'

'Did too.'

'Shut *uuup*!'

'See? It's like he's here anyway,' said Max, tugging Ripley's hand. 'Come on. You can choose the channel if you like.'

They sat on the sofa and turned the TV up extra loud, as if it was a treat that Dad wasn't home. Max got the armchair all to himself. Thelma had three bowls of Krispies for breakfast, with two spoons of sugar on each.

But there was a fluttering feeling in Max's chest that wouldn't let him enjoy it.

Half an hour went past; then an hour; and Dad wasn't back.

Louise sat curled on the sofa reading her book, but every now and then she looked at the clock and stole a glance at Max, and he knew she was thinking it too.

Then Thelma pinched the remote and changed the channel to something about cooking chicken in wine, and Ripley screamed and pulled her hair, which made Thelma kick out and knock Louise's book from her hand hard enough to rip a page, so Max had a lot of yelling to do.

But it just covered up the fluttery feeling. It didn't make it go away.

Max went to the bedroom. Dad had given them mobile phones: one to Max, a big blocky one with buttons and no touchscreen like his own, which Max broke three days later; one to Thelma, which she lost even more quickly and entirely on purpose due to 'the shame'; and one to Louise, who hoarded its pre-paid calls 'for emergencies', like she was supposed to.

Max pulled it from under her pillow and called Dad's mobile.

There was a buzzing from the front room, and the tinkly notes of a ringtone.

'Max!' yelled Thelma.

When he arrived, Louise was holding Dad's mobile, still ringing.

'It was down the side of the sofa,' she said, her face pale.

'He's just forgotten it,' said Max, as if saying that would make it feel true. He snatched the phone out of her hand and put it on the table.

Ripley crawled into Max's arms, cuddling Potato between them.

'Where's he gone, Max?' she whispered into his neck. 'When's he coming back?'

Max thought about what Dad would do if he was here, which was daft because if he was then he wouldn't have to do anything. But what Dad would do would be to take everyone off somewhere different, as a distraction. Like an Anti-Reflection Room, so that the last thing you had time to do was think. The day of Mum's funeral they'd come home and played *Twister* and *Buckaroo* and *KerPlunk*, all day, and they'd laughed and laughed. And this wasn't the same, definitely; it definitely completely wasn't. But it still seemed like a good idea.

So Max took them to Fallowfield again.

Max took Ripley to the pet shop. It was massive, and smelled of straw and oats and the outdoors. It made Max's nose itch.

Ripley went straight to the back, where they kept the rabbits. There were three perfect snowy-white ones, babies, all quivery in one pen. In the pen next door, there was another one, by itself: fat and squat with one flopped-over ear, and splotchy brown fur.

'That one,' said Ripley, inevitably, pointing at the squat splotchy rabbit. 'Cos it's a bit crap. I bet it's been here ages. I bet no one else wants it.'

They looked at hutches too, but the cheapest one to go indoors was thirty pounds. Ripley blinked at the price, tracing it with her finger and crinkling her twenty-pound note between her fingers.

Max groaned.

'I'll pay the extra,' he said. 'We can't have a rabbit without a hutch, right?'

Ripley sniffed. 'It's OK. I bet we don't need a hutch. We could just give it a box to sleep in. Or the bottom of a cupboard. The rest of the time it could just run about.'

But it turned out you couldn't just buy a rabbit anyway, not without an adult to say you were allowed.

'Bye bye, Blueberry Muffins,' said Ripley sadly, waving as they left.

Denny's Sporting Goods was next door. Max pressed his face up against the window, and stared at the pure white trainers. They were reduced again: fifty pounds now.

'You can't have my money,' said Ripley. 'I'm not as nice as you.'

They met the twins in the car park.

Thelma had bought a rubber in the shape of a flamingo. 'Llamas are so over. Everyone likes flamingos now.'

Louise had bought a large notebook with a bumpy green cover, like leather, or dragon-skin.

Dad wasn't back when they got home.

He wasn't back for tea. Max made fish fingers and oven chips and beans.

He wasn't back when Ripley went to bed, or the twins.

'He'll be at work now,' said Max. 'It's like any other night.'

Max stayed up watching the TV on volume twenty-three, just because.

Then he went to sleep in his bunk, because it wasn't different from any other night, because Dad was always at work by now, and maybe he'd just done a double shift, and he definitely hadn't been hit by a car and killed instantly, definitely not.

Max was having a dream about Disneyland, and there being a huge accident where a rollercoaster fell to bits in the middle of a ride, and everyone was shouting 'He did it!' and pointing at Max, even though he was waiting innocently in the queue to go on it like everyone else – when a hand covered his mouth.

'Max. Wake up, Max,' whispered a voice in the darkness.

'Dad,' whispered Max against the palm of the hand.

'Shhh.'

The hand disappeared. Max lifted his head, blinking, as the image of Dad's face slowly grew clearer.

'Where –?'

Dad held a finger to Max's lips.

'Quiet, Max. Listen up. There's a bit of trouble. I need you to hold the fort for a few days.'

*I did*, thought Max. *I made fish fingers and oven chips and beans, and we didn't even buy a rabbit.*

'Step up, Max. Take care of the girls, just till I'm back.'

He tucked something under Max's pillow.

Then he touched Max on the top of his head, nodded, and vanished.

Max went back to sleep, because Dad was probably just a weird extra bit of a dream.

But in the morning, he felt a knotty lump under his pillow, and there it was.

A roll of twenty-pound notes, tied with an elastic band.

# 4

'How much is there?' asked Thelma, her eyes wide behind her glasses.

They were all gathered in the front room on Sunday morning, staring at the scattered twenties on the coffee table.

'Two hundred quid,' said Max.

Earlier, when his hand had touched the roll of notes, firmly coiled in their rubber band, it had all rushed back. Not a dream after all: Dad was OK, and Max was in charge, and now they were *rich*.

'Where's he gone, though?' asked Louise, frowning.

'It's a secret, dummy,' said Ripley.

'He doesn't have to keep it a secret from *us*,' said Louise, her frown getting deeper.

Max reckoned she had a point, but he rolled his eyes anyway. 'It's just a few days, right? That's what he said. It'll be fine.'

He furled the notes back up into a tight bundle and slipped them into his pocket.

Then he went round to see Elis Evans.

'There's fresh paint up there,' said Elis Evans's mum. 'So no accidents today, right, Max?'

'I'll be dead careful,' said Max, putting his old trainers in the porch.

Upstairs, Elis Evans was sitting by a bright blue wall in a room that smelled of paint, gluing two pieces of wood together.

'I'm building a swift box,' he said. 'To replace their natural habitat.'

Max had been going to tell Elis Evans about Dad, and how he was in charge now. But now he was here, in the freshly painted bedroom a world away from Nice Jackie's boxes, it seemed like a secret he should keep.

He let Elis Evans talk instead, about how birds liked pastry much more than bread, and how you could be a hunting-eagle trainer at their age if you grew up in Mongolia. Then Max got bored and threw one of Elis Evans's model birds to see if it would fly, which it could, right into the fresh blue paintwork. Its wing left a thin deep scratch of white.

Elis Evans said his bed would probably go there anyway, so it didn't matter.

Even Elis Evans's mum seemed to like him more than usual today.

'You take this back for the girls, will you?' she said as he left, pressing a tin into his hand, weighty with cake.

'Give them my love. They'd be welcome round for tea, you know. If they'd like.'

That was just how it was when you were rich, Max reckoned. The minute you didn't need it, people just handed you stuff.

He carried the cake tin slung under one arm, one hand in his pocket on the bundle of notes. He could get more fish fingers on the way back: posh ones. He could buy Ripley that rabbit. And flamingo junk for Thelma, and dragon books for Louise. He could buy anything.

He had to walk past Denny's Sporting Goods on the way.

There were the pure white trainers in the window.

*Final Reduction: £49.*

Max pressed his hands against the window, and felt a longing worse than ever. Before, he was never going to have those trainers; not really, like he wasn't ever going to wake up in a world where people called Max didn't have to go to school. Some stuff was just fantasy. But now there was money in his pocket, and he could, he really could, he could just walk in there and –

He should try them on, at least.

The man at the counter looked surprised. 'In the window? Oh yeah. Those are last year's, you know that? Model Five comes out next week . . . we'll have them for ninety-nine pounds, one week only . . .'

Max shook his head. These were the ones he wanted.

He wanted them even more once they were on his feet. His old trainers were grey and bent, and there was a worn place in the right one where you could feel the pavement. These were like gloves, so white they almost glowed, and with a springiness under his feet like he was on the moon.

'That is the *final* reduction,' said the man, as Max fingered the price tag.

'I'll take them,' said Max breathlessly. 'Don't put them back in the box. I'll wear them now.'

Max let the man put his sad grey trainers in the bin, and practically floated all the way home.

Until he arrived to find the front door wide open, and a police officer in the hallway.

# 5

Max felt all his breath leave his body. Police meant bad news: *the* bad news, the worst news.

Dad.

He sagged against the wall. But Thelma ran into the hallway, and he could see from her furious face behind the officer that this was a different kind of bad.

'They just came in, Max!' she said, frightened as well as angry. 'And now they're turning over all our stuff!'

'Good afternoon – Max, is it?' said the officer. She had long dark hair twirled into a knobbly knot at the base of her neck, and a wide but unfriendly smile. 'I'm PC Farhi. We didn't just come in, actually – we knocked, and your little sister opened the door. Very sweet of her. So we thought we'd have a look round, while we're here.'

There was a thump in the bedroom followed by an anguished wail from Louise. When Max pushed his way in, there was another police officer, pulling all the Dragonslayer Chronicles books out from under Louise's bunk and shaking them by the cover.

'It's your dad we'd like to talk to really, Max,' said PC Farhi, in a honey-sweet voice. 'Piotr Kowalski?'

*Pee-yot-er*, she said it, when it was just Peter, in Polish. Just Big Pete.

'He's in a bit of trouble, see. Just tell us where we can find him and we'll leave right now.'

Max felt cool fresh sweat across his back.

But he pushed the panic down, out of sight. He pulled his shoulders back, trying to look taller.

'You can leave right now anyway,' Max said. 'Unless you've got a search warrant?'

It was what they said on TV, when they had something to hide.

PC Farhi narrowed her eyes. 'Chip off the old block, aren't you?'

Max nodded. 'That's me.'

'Reckon we'll be seeing each other again then, kid. Come on, PC Draper, time to go!'

The officer dropped the book she was holding on to the floor, to another wail from Louise.

Max followed them to the door, and closed it with a hard bang to make sure they were on the other side. Then he rested his head against it, just for a moment.

'Oh, Max,' sniffed Louise. 'That was just – they were just –'

'Meanies,' said Ripley, her face stained with tears.

'You were brilliant, though,' said Thelma. 'Search warrant? Brilliant.'

Max didn't feel brilliant. He felt sick. With relief that they hadn't asked him to turn out his pockets. With relief that it wasn't – that. The other reason the police knocked at your door: *there's been an accident, you'd better come to the hospital, you'd better come now.*

Dad was fine. He was in a bit of trouble, but he'd sort it. He always did.

'They won't be back,' said Max, with confidence. 'It's probably mistaken identity, innit.'

'Wait. Have you got new trainers?' asked Thelma.

And suddenly Max wasn't brilliant any more. Max was mean too, and sneaky, and, like, totally unfair.

He promised them shopping at Fallowfield for whatever they wanted most in the world – except for a rabbit – and let them eat the whole cake from Mrs Evans's tin, in thick crumby wedges.

Max had forgotten the rest of the shopping, so they followed the cake up with delivery pizza: fat droopy slices, with no mushrooms because Max was in charge and what he said went. They'd still put little green herbs on it that he had to pick off. But it was all good. The girls were happy. He'd got rid of the police, for now at least. And Dad would be back soon.

'I like being rich,' said Thelma, with her mouth full.

Max looked at his trainers.

Yep. He could get used to it.

# 6

On Monday, Max put on his uniform and walked the girls to school as usual. Then came straight back home.

This wasn't a day for school. This was a day for staying home, on guard.

Besides, Dad would probably be back today, and Max wanted to be the first to see him.

He watched Mrs Gupta pass the window on her way to Sainsbury's, pushing little Anil, who cried. Then he peeled a few notes off the bundle of twenties, wrapped the rest in an old sock, and buried it in the hard cold earth of her yucca plant. The police would never look there, and the earthworm wouldn't mind.

Maybe, if he left it there long enough, the money would grow. Tiny coins, that started as pennies and grew up to be pounds. Damp pale notes, unfurling like leaves. Like a bank, but natural.

Then he went inside and sat in the dim of the morning with the curtains drawn, looking at Dad's mobile phone.

Dad could call it. He knew the number. Maybe he left it on purpose, so he could call it, and Max would answer, and he'd hear Dad say, 'Big man! How's it going? Well done. I'm picking up dinner on the way home.'

Dad's phone started ringing, and Max picked it up so fast he almost dropped it – but it wasn't Dad. It was Paul, from the yard, wondering why Big Pete hadn't turned up for his shift in the forklift that morning.

'Off sick,' said Max quickly, knowing that was what Dad would say if he'd messed up his shifts and needed time off to work at the club.

Paul sounded unimpressed.

'He needs to call that in. You tell him,' he said, and hung up.

Then Max called school, in a deep voice with his hand over the phone to muffle it, telling them Max was sick too.

It was too quiet in the flat by himself.

Max went out into the estate, Dad's phone tucked in one pocket, cash in the other.

The bright Christmas lights dappling Seaview Tower were cheerful: a reindeer, a snowflake, flashing reds and yellows in star shapes all across one balcony. There was an inflatable snowman tethered in one corner, its broad belly rippling in the wind.

They should have one of those. He could buy one, now they were rich. They could cover the walkway in sparkling lights that twinkled like snow falling, and a tree, a real one, so tall you had to saw the top off like Elis Evans had one year.

They were due a real Christmas. The first year after Mum, it had been too fresh, and the day had passed with stilted attempts at joy that stubbornly would not come when called. Last year, Dad had tried his best. But they were skint, and their thin stockings were filled with plastic toys that broke, and cherry liqueur chocolates that Dad had been given a crate of by a mate. Max could still remember the crack of the sugar crust inside and the burning too-ripe sweetness of cherry brandy: the same going down as when it came back up.

This year would be different.

He resisted the guy selling trees all wound up in red netting, and walked past the tinsel and lights in the big supermarket. But he went to the little shop on the corner and bought three chocolate Santas, because rich people didn't have to wait for Christmas stockings for those.

At home, he put some laundry in the machine, with a bit of washing-up liquid because there wasn't any powder, and he didn't want to go out again, just in case.

Then he watched TV in fits and starts until it was time to pick up the girls from school.

They were huddled in a hopeful clump in the yard, waiting.

'Is he –?' asked Louise, in a whisper.

'Not yet,' said Max, as if it was all as he'd expected.

They had pizza for dinner again. Ripley fell asleep on the sofa with a slice still in her hand, and he carried her, snoring, into her bunk.

Max wasn't good at much. Every teacher he'd ever had had made that pretty clear. But Max wasn't bad at this. He was stepping up. He was being the big man, a chip off the old block; Big Pete Kowalski's little twin. If Dad had been here to see it, that's what he'd say.

And he'd be back soon, to say it.

He'd be back soon.

# 7

Dad didn't come back on Tuesday.

Max phoned school: off sick again, oh dear, then kept the mobile phone plugged in and fully charged as he stayed home from school waiting, all day.

Max dipped into the sock buried deep and hopeful in the yucca plant pot, and bought fish fingers and oven chips and washing powder.

Max told the girls it was fine, despite the uneasy but certain sense beneath his skin that it was not.

'I don't think this is OK, Max,' whispered Louise on Wednesday morning, too worried even to read her book while eating her Krispies. 'He's missing. He's definitely a missing person.'

'What if he went in a hole and broke himself?' said Ripley, her eyes big.

'Why would he have gone in a hole?' asked Thelma.

'People go in holes,' Ripley said seriously. 'All the time.'

She discovered her hair was in her breakfast bowl, and licked the ends.

'He could live for two weeks without food, but only three days without water,' said Louise, thoughtfully stirring her spoon. 'Unless he's injured, of course. Shock can be fatal.'

'Shut up!' yelled Max, grabbing her ponytail and pulling.

Louise leaped up with a howl, spilling milk and bloated Krispies across the sofa and all over Ripley's school socks.

Ripley began to wail.

'You shut up and all!'

'No, you!' shouted Thelma, pushing him in the shoulder.

Max stumbled, then recovered and lunged at her, and they fought until Max pushed her hard – hard enough to fling her backwards. Her head hit the wall with a thump. She yelped, and slid to the floor, clutching at the back of her head.

'Look what you did!' shouted Louise.

'I'm all wet,' whimpered Ripley, sitting in a puddle on the sofa.

It was too loud, and too much. Max put his hands over his ears and shut his eyes tightly, turning to the wall. It was quiet there. It was away. He went away, in his head.

The girls were upset. He was in charge, and the girls were upset.

He felt buzzy, as if something was drumming in his blood.

'Max!' said Louise sharply.

46

He kept his eyes shut.

'Max, look!'

When he opened his eyes, she was beside him, thrusting Dad's mobile phone under his nose. At the top of the screen there was a small symbol: two circles on a line.

Voicemail.

'Why didn't it ring?'

'You had it on silent, Max,' Louise said quietly.

Max couldn't have felt worse if she'd yelled it. He'd missed the call. He'd kept the phone charged, but somehow he'd turned off the ringer. Max Kowalski, the idiot king.

Max snatched the phone and dialled for the message at once, heart in his mouth.

*You have one new message.*

'Hiya, kids. Guess who?'

It was Dad. Dad's warm voice, full of laughs. His dad.

Max held his hand up, telling them to stay quiet. He needed to listen. He pressed the phone tight to his ear.

'Reckoned this was the best way to catch up, yeah? Just checking in. I'm away a bit longer than I thought, but it's all OK, right? Back soon. I promise. Max: you keep looking after those girls, big man. Step up, yeah? I'm counting on you. Angels: behave yourselves. Princess: love you, baby, be good. Oh – and don't call back, you hear? Not on this number. It's important, Max. Don't call me back on this number. I'll call you. Soon. Right –'

There was a noise of another voice, far off, and Dad shouting something back, his mouth turned away. Then the call ended.

Max put it on speaker and played it again, so they could all hear.

Dad was OK. Dad was OK, and coming back in a few days.

Max's finger hovered over the stored number, the one he was not meant to call back. He longed to press it. To tell him about the fish fingers, and the police, and hear his dad tell him how proud he was.

But there wasn't time. He had to get Ripley changed. He had to be nice to Thelma on the way to school, while Louise babbled on about checking people for head wounds and the signs of concussion.

Back at the flat, he had to mop up all the mess.

The sofa wasn't ever going to be the same again. But the girls were happy. That was all that mattered.

Dad didn't come back on Thursday, or on Friday.

On Friday, before he picked up the girls, Max dipped into the yucca plant pot again, taking the lot with him. Then he took them all shopping at Fallowfield, like he'd promised.

'It's early Christmas!' said Ripley.

'Christmas is cancelled,' grumped Thelma, kicking a bin.

It wasn't. The estate had seemed so brightly Christmassy. But at Fallowfield, Christmas seemed to vibrate in the air, across the walls in glitter and fluff, in sparkle and sticky-fingered desire. The walkways were hung with golden trees and giant baubles, gently buffeted by the air conditioning. The air echoed with Christmas songs. And there were people, so many people: carrying six bags in each hand, clutching lists, tugging on the arms of wailing children with smeary faces.

Max shuddered as the noise built in his ears. He hated busy places. He'd got lost once, when he was little, in among the long skirts and shiny rails and hundreds of people. Mum had been by his side and then suddenly she was gone. Just gone.

He felt it sometimes, when he woke up, and remembered: that same lost boy's panic.

But he had his white trainers, and he'd promised.

Thelma bought a flamingo backpack, on which all the flamingos were wearing Santa hats.

Louise got a fountain pen, the kind with a gold nib, and a box of ink cartridges, 'because real writers don't use biros'.

Ripley spent what seemed like an hour by the rabbits, pining for the now-adopted Blueberry Muffins for the briefest of moments before falling in love with a runty lop she named Buttery Toast. Then she bought a silver plastic tiara with yellow and blue jewels on it, and wore it out of the shop.

After, they went to the beach, and braved the brutal cold wind while they had chips on the wall again. Chips, and doughnuts, and two goes each on whatever they wanted, and everyone was happy, so happy, so like he wanted them all to be. Like Dad would want.

When they got home, Max sat on the sofa by himself and emptied out the money that was left.

It wasn't healthy and fat and fed by the soil.

It wasn't a roll at all.

It was six pounds and seven p.

That was it. That was all they had in the whole world. They'd been rich, and now they weren't.

Max wiggled his toes in his pure white trainers and felt a glow of shame come to his cheeks.

He was in charge.

And he'd messed up.

# 8

The problem with sisters, Max thought, was that if there was a thing you didn't want them to know, you had no chance.

'Max! There's no milk!'

'There's no Krispies left either.'

'Or bread.'

'Or butter.'

'Can *I* have new trainers?'

That was Ripley, wearing his and walking like a penguin.

'No,' said Max, pulling the pillow over his head.

He knew why Dad liked his Saturday morning lie-ins now.

'Max. Max. Max. *Maaaax!*'

That was Thelma, poking his pillow with a flamingo pencil.

He managed to ignore them for most of the morning. Until Thelma reappeared, having taken their last six pounds and seven p to the One Stop, and spent most of it on a magazine that had free plastic flamingo sunglasses stuck to the front.

Max shouted at her, and threw his pillow at her, and Potato, and he would've thrown something else too if it had been handy.

'But we're rich!' Thelma shouted back, readjusting her flamingo sunglasses.

'No, we're not!'

And then it all came out.

'I thought you were spending too much money,' said Louise, looking up from her book, 'when you were spending it. I just didn't like to say.'

They had the rest of Thelma's shopping: milk, a box of Krispies, and some midget gems.

A tin of beans in the cupboard.

A scrape of margarine in the fridge.

And nothing else.

Nothing, till Dad came home.

Max put the TV on, and let them each have a turn of the remote to watch whatever they wanted.

They had Krispies for lunch. Small bowls.

They watched more TV, until it grew dark outside.

They had Krispies for dinner too.

'What are we going to do now, Max?' asked Louise.

'Eat the midget gems?' said Ripley. 'To make us feel better?'

'I ate them already,' said Thelma. 'Sorry.'

Louise fixed Max with serious eyes. 'Max. I think – I think we need to call someone. We need help.'

Kowalskis never asked for help.

You looked after yourself. You looked after your family. And you didn't need anything or anyone else.

'No,' said Max. 'Dad'll come.'

'What if he doesn't?' whispered Louise, putting her hands over Ripley's ears.

Thelma looked grim. 'Then we'll be stuck in some children's home forever.'

'We won't,' said Max, at once.

'We will. We'll go to school on Monday, all sad and starved, and they'll call the police, and we'll go into care. We'll be those sad children on adverts who need to get adopted, only we're too old and no one'll want us. And we'll probably all be sent to live in different places because there's four of us, and four is loads, and we'll never see each other again until we're reunited when we're really ancient and crinkly on *Long Lost Family* with Davina.'

'No, we won't!' wailed Ripley. 'Will we? At *Christmas*?'

'I told you,' said Thelma. 'Christmas is cancelled.'

'That won't happen!' said Louise. 'Will it, Max?'

She knotted her hands in her hair and Max realized she wasn't asking for Ripley. She was asking for herself.

Max thought of the handful of coins they had left now, and felt sick.

He thought of school too, and felt stupid. They didn't like it if you were off for more than three days without a note. He'd called in sick every day, putting on his deep voice, but he wasn't sure it would be enough.

There was probably a social worker assigned to their case already. And if they came round now . . .

Max looked around the flat.

There was the empty fish-finger packet on top of the bin, because the bin itself was full of pizza boxes and Max hated taking it out because the big bin was tall, and Max was not tall, not yet; he would be but not yet. There was the grill pan on the oven, covered in burnt crumbs, and all their plates with smeary ketchup. Dirty breakfast bowls in an uneven tower. That load of washing he'd put on, still in the machine.

Suddenly he was glad Dad wasn't here to see it.

Thelma was right: if anyone came to check on them now, they'd be packed off to some care home for children. Babcia and Dziadek had died before the twins were born. They'd only met Uncle Tomasz once, and he lived in Gdansk. Mum didn't have a family; not the kind she'd chosen to share with the one she'd made. There was no one but Dad.

There was a tap at the front door.

They all fell still.

Then there was the scrape of a key in the lock.

Max's heart gave a mighty leap in his chest.

'Hello hello, anyone at home?'

It dropped like a stone.

Not Big Pete Kowalski, home at last.

It was Nice Jackie, letting herself in with a key Max didn't know she had.

'All right, my sweeties?'

She appeared in a haze of sweet vanilla perfume. She was younger than Dad even though he worked for her, and delicate: small hands with pink nails, a slight frame. She wore an oversized and expensive-looking white coat with fluff at the collar and cuffs, white boots and a pink dress that stopped above her knee. Her hair was honey blonde and shiny. Her eyes were painted all round in black, with long dark lashes.

Nice Jackie gave Max a glossy pink smile, rolling a bright pink suitcase on wheels into view.

'Auntie Jackie's here!'

Ripley climbed behind Max in his armchair. 'Who's Auntie Jackie?'

Max had never heard her called that before, to be honest. But he remembered the glass of Coke with the ice and the straw, and he got up so she could have the best chair.

'Your daddy works for me, sweetheart,' said Nice Jackie, giving Ripley's cheek a pinch as she sat down. 'I gave him a job, when he was struggling. He's like family now. Which means you are too. Got to look after each other, don't we? Pete asked me to check up on you, make sure you were doing OK.'

She looked round the room, her nose crinkling faintly in distaste at the bin smell.

'When?' asked Max.

'Where is he?' asked Thelma.

Nice Jackie smiled again, smoothing her skirt. 'Away,' she said sweetly, not looking at Thelma. 'We've had a bit of trouble. At work. So he's lying low. Visiting friends, till it cools off.'

Max frowned. He knew all Dad's friends. Paul from the factory. Radek and Abdi from the club. Anna and her daughter Katya, who babysat them once and only once. They all lived in Southend. They were all just around the corner. And Dad was . . . somewhere else.

'Mistaken identity, you said,' whispered Louise, looking at Max.

'But he's OK?' demanded Thelma again.

'He isn't in a hole?' asked Ripley.

Nice Jackie laughed, a high tinkling sound. 'No. *He's* fine.' She drummed her nails on the hard plastic of the suitcase.

'Have you come to stay with us?' asked Louise, in a small voice.

Max felt a moment's guilty relief at the thought. A grown-up, to help him out. Not to take over. Just to help.

Nice Jackie laughed thinly. 'No, sweetheart.'

'Then what's the suitcase for?'

Nice Jackie smiled at Max again.

'Max is going to look after it for me, aren't you, sweetie?'

She stood up, and wheeled the case over to him, bumping it up against his feet.

'Pete always talks about you. All of you: his princess, his angels, his big man – just like his dad. Now's your chance to prove it, eh, Max?'

Max liked the sound of that.

'How?' he said.

Nice Jackie nodded at the pink suitcase.

'You're going to look after my stuff for a few days; just till things quiet down a bit. My boys will be along to pick the case up. Like before, Max. You remember? You'll be paid, of course. I always pay my boys well.'

It was as if she knew what they needed, Max thought. As if the whole universe knew, and for once had decided to be on his side.

'Course,' said Max, squaring his shoulders, all business, as if he did this kind of thing all the time.

'Good boy,' said Nice Jackie, cupping his cheek.

She dipped into her bag, and pulled out a few notes, tucking them into his jeans.

'More where that came from,' she cooed.

Then she clicked away, banging the door closed behind her.

The sweetness of vanilla hung in the air.

The pink suitcase stood at Max's feet. Its brightness looked odd and out of place in their scruffy front room: a hard plastic case on wheels, with clips to hold it shut.

'What do you think's in it?' asked Thelma.

'More rabbits?' asked Ripley hopefully.

'None of our business,' said Louise. 'You can't go opening other people's bags.'

'You can if they tell you to look after them,' said Thelma. 'Cos it could be anything. There might be a bomb in it.'

'Max?' asked Ripley.

'There isn't a bomb in it, Ripley.'

'Are you sure, though?' asked Thelma, grinning.

That was that, then. Now he had to check or he'd never get any peace.

Max laid the case down on its back, unclipped the catches, then sat on the sofa staring at the contents with his mouth open.

Not rabbits.

Not bottles of vodka or packets of cigarettes.

Money.

Cash.

Used bank notes, thousands of them, in neat fat stacks.

# 9

'Are we rich again?' asked Ripley.

'Yes!' said Thelma.

'No!' said Louise. 'It's not ours!'

It wasn't theirs. It was Nice Jackie's.

Nice Jackie's suitcase full of money, in their front room.

'Why would she give it to us?' asked Ripley, reaching one licked finger out to touch the money.

Max slapped her hand away and flipped the suitcase closed, hard.

He knew why.

This wasn't the sort of money you put in a bank. This was the sort of money you got from boxes you took away in the night; boxes filled with bottles of vodka and cigarettes with unfamiliar names. And the police had already searched the flat. So now it would be safe here.

Max swallowed. He was used to being in trouble: the Reflection Room, and detentions, and having to say sorry to Elis Evans's mum. But this was different. This was the real kind of trouble. The kind where people get hurt. The kind that Dad had run away from.

And now Max had opened the lid on a whole lot more.

'Go to bed,' he said. 'Go. Now. No arguments. Just go to bed. I need to think.'

Max sat quietly on the sofa for a time, listening to Ripley's light snores; wondering how many times Dad had sat awake here doing just the same.

He should be here. He'd know what to do. He wouldn't be scared; not Big Pete Kowalski. He'd be brave and bold.

Max felt anything but.

He could still see the edge of the case, peeping from behind the chair.

He escaped outside, on to the third-floor passage running along past all the front doors. He breathed in the sharp cold of the night, welcoming the chill on his skin.

He looked out across the tall blocks of flats and the squat rows of houses, all fighting to win the Christmas contest. The dazzle and flash of *Merry Christmas* from one house with every window framed in lights and a Santa up a ladder climbing on the roof. The inflatable snowman on Seaview Tower, which was losing its puff, its top hat sagging.

He tried calling the forbidden number, but hung up after one ring, too scared of who might answer.

'I need you, Dad,' he said into the darkness. He let the words out softly, like a message that might carry. 'I need some help.'

He caught a snatch of 'Fairytale of New York' as big kids in Santa hats sang and laughed as they ran past the One Stop, wearing tinsel for scarves.

He wished he was down there with them, mucking about. He wanted their flat to be all lights and snowmen and looking forward to Christmas.

But he couldn't have that.

And he couldn't keep waiting for his dad.

So he had to make what he did have work.


Max didn't sleep.

On Sunday morning, he went round to Elis Evans's house.

'Hello, love, you're early,' said Elis Evans's mum. Then she took one look at Max's top, sighed, and pulled it right off him. 'Men. Honestly.'

Max stood bare-chested in Elis Evans's kitchen, crossing his arms over his front awkwardly as she threw it into the machine. He was going to be big, he was going to be six foot three; he wasn't yet, though, so she might not know. She turned, her face softening.

'I'm putting a wash on anyway, Max. Could put the rest in too . . .?'

Max looked down at his socks – the same ones he'd worn since Wednesday, were they? – and at his jeans, but shook his head.

She smiled, and pushed an ironed striped T-shirt and a knitted jumper covered in squirrels into his shivering arms.

'Go on. They'll be a bit big on you, but they'll do.'

They smelled of clean; of home and care and time and love. They smelled like his old life. He pulled them both over his head, squirming at the feel of the tags scratching at his shoulders.

His mum always cut them out, whenever Max got new clothes. And she must have told Elis Evans's mum one time, because she reached behind him with a pair of scissors and snipped those labels out, at once, without a word.

Max felt a big wall of something stopping up his throat.

Elis Evans's mum looked at him and tilted her head, and he ran away upstairs before the hug could begin.

Elis Evans was sitting on the long table in his bedroom, surrounded by tiny clay birds and pots of paint. There were swans and swifts, robins and kingfishers, and a few that had, perhaps, not turned out quite as birdlike as intended. Elis Evans was painting them with a tiny thin brush.

Max climbed on to the table too.

'Nice jumper,' said Elis Evans, barely looking up.

'Borrowed it off some nerdy kid,' said Max.

'You should keep it. He's probably a bit over squirrels.'

There was a tiny china dragon on the table too, curled up and sleeping. It had two keys hanging off it on a thin silver chain.

'That's the keys to my nain's house, in Wales,' said Elis Evans, when Max picked them up. 'I was going to paint the dragon too. It's meant to be gold, though, and I haven't got gold.'

The dragon was cool in Max's hand. It was mostly white, but you could see in places where the gold paint was not quite worn away. It had a chip in its long narrow head where a porcelain ear had broken off, and the missing part was rough against his thumb. The words *Tŷ Gwyn* were etched into the base, in a childish hand. But the rest was smooth and solid, with nubbly bumps along the spine and the tail. He held it, feeling it grow warm in his palm.

'You can help, if you like. I'm trying to build a menagerie of a hundred. Then I'm going to hang them on our Christmas tree. We're getting a Nordmann fir this afternoon. The one at my dad's house has been up for two weeks already, but Mum says that's because he's uncivilized.'

Elis Evans passed him a tiny paintbrush. Max picked up a robin, its breast already painted red, and blobbed a bit of brown across its back. But the paint came off on his fingers where he held it, and smudged the red.

He tried again with another one, but the paint was too wet, and dribbled.

'Try the swan,' said Elis Evans, pushing one towards Max. 'It's only the beak, really.'

Max stared at it. He didn't want to paint a swan because he was too useless to do a robin.

He didn't want to do any of it.

He tried really hard and it didn't matter; it never seemed to matter.

The wall of something was back in his throat. Only this time it wouldn't go away. This time it rose up and choked him and lit a fire in his nose and suddenly he was crying.

He could feel Elis Evans watching him and he dragged his squirrel-jumper sleeve across his face, trying to scrape off all the feelings as well as the snot. He hadn't come here for this. He'd had a plan of what to say, and how to say it. But the feeling wouldn't stop. It was as if now it had stepped out of him, it was too large to go back in.

Elis Evans very quietly got up and closed the door. He placed a box of tissues on the desk, quite casually, as if they might be needed one of these days. Then he climbed back on to the table and went on painting.

'My dad didn't come home this week,' Max said.

'Oh,' said Elis Evans, dipping his brush into the black paint.

'I bought new trainers and I took the girls out and we ran out of money and now –'

Now Max was scared, really scared: for Dad, for all of them.

'I don't think . . . I don't think I can fix it.'

Elis Evans painted quietly for a while.

'Do you want me to tell my mum?' he said eventually, putting down his brush.

Max felt shame wash over him the instant the words were spoken.

It was so kind, and so what he had hoped for. A small film had been playing in the back of his skull: living here, with the big fridge and someone else to get the knots out of Ripley's hair. Sharing Elis Evans's big bedroom. Having someone else in charge.

*We need help*, Max said in the film in his head.

*I can see that*, said Mrs Evans, *and you should all live with me for just a little while, and here's a biscuit.*

But Kowalskis didn't ask for help.

Besides, Mrs Evans liked Max. She wouldn't like him if he brought the pink suitcase into her house.

And she'd never liked Dad. If she knew he'd disappeared, just left them to cope alone – he couldn't let that happen.

Max sniffed, and shook his head. 'Nah. It's a secret. And – and I've got a plan, actually,' he added, suddenly, before he could stop himself. 'I've got a really good plan. Forget I said anything.'

When Max left to go home, he was still wearing the squirrel jumper.

Mrs Evans pressed a tin of cake into his hands.

And in Max's pocket slept a small curled dragon, and a stolen pair of keys to a house in Wales.

## 10

'Wales? Why would we go to *Wales*?' asked Thelma, crunching up her face.

Because if they stayed social services would come, Max thought.

Because there was a suitcase of money in their flat, and police looking for it – and if they found it, Dad would be in even more trouble. Max too.

'Because that's where the house is,' he said instead.

Elis Evans's nain's cottage in Wales, that she was selling because she lived in a home now. Elis Evans's nain's cottage, that was empty, and waiting for them.

Elis Evans wouldn't mind that Max had stolen the keys; not really. It wouldn't even be for long. Just till Dad came back.

'How will Dad know where we've gone?' asked Ripley.

Thelma sniffed. 'He should've thought of that. Serve him right if he comes back and worries cos he doesn't know where we are.'

Ripley's eyes went wide.

'She doesn't mean it, Rips,' said Max firmly. 'We've got Louise's phone, haven't we? So we'll take it with us. And when he's back, he can phone it and we'll tell him.'

'What about Christmas?'

'He'll be back by then,' Max said confidently.

Of course he would. He wouldn't leave them over Christmas. It was the sixteenth of December: loads of time.

'What about school?' asked Louise.

'There's only one week left till the holidays. No one'll mind.'

He waited for Louise to complain that she couldn't possibly lie to a teacher. But her eyes were sparkling.

'We can each pack our own bags,' she said. 'I'll sort out food, and bathroom things. Ripley, you should pack some toys and books. Max – you can work out how we get there.' She beamed. 'It's like an adventure, a proper adventure.'

It wasn't, really. Max reckoned a proper adventure would have a magic teleporter, or a free limousine on the doorstep to drive them. Trains to Wales, it turned out, weren't cheap.

'That's stealing,' said Ripley, when Max clicked open the case and took out a few bundles.

'Nah,' said Max, trying to sound confident while feeling anything but. 'She was going to pay me anyway, right?'

He guiltily clicked the case shut, and added it to the pile of bags by the front.

She'd asked them to look after it. So that's what he would do – in Wales. And when she found a way to bring Dad home, she could have it back.

They left in the dark, and early. Four children with backpacks and a bright pink suitcase, on a Monday morning in the middle of December, with no adult in sight: that was going to raise eyebrows.

Max had made them rehearse it all the way to the station.

'Our dad's just in the shop, getting a paper.'

'We go to a posh school where the holidays start early.'

'We're going to visit our granny in North Wales.'

And in case of total emergency: 'I'm not allowed to talk to strangers.'

He need not have worried. The woman at the ticket desk took so long to understand Max's attempts to stand on tiptoe and shout 'Four singles to Betws-y-Coed,' into her microphone that she didn't seem fussed about him sliding a fat stack of cash over the counter. And on the train into London, and on the Tube, no one looked at anyone else. It was as if they were all running away too.

At Euston, they climbed on to a long train, and claimed a table – four seats together – and glared at anyone who looked at them twice.

'Need a hand with that?' asked a tall man in glasses, eyeing the pink suitcase. 'There are overhead racks for luggage.'

Max had the case balanced awkwardly on his lap, wedged up against the table, with one arm wrapped round it.

'No thanks,' said Max, gripping it firmly.

'We go to a posh school,' said Louise hopefully.

The man blinked. Then he smiled politely, and settled into his seat.

'Are we nearly there?' asked Ripley, after the train had been moving for three minutes.

Max groaned. It would take seven hours, they'd said, when he phoned. A train, a Tube, a train, a train, a bus. Seven hours at least of *Are we nearly there yet?*

'We're not even in the right country yet, Rips,' said Louise. 'Why don't you get out some colouring or something? It's going to be ages.'

But it turned out Ripley's tightly hugged backpack contained Potato the stuffed rabbit, and nothing else.

'Don't look at me,' said Thelma, clutching her flamingo pencil case and scooping her flamingo notebook off the table. 'These aren't for sharing.'

Louise pretended to be too busy reading her book to have noticed.

So they played I-Spy, which with Ripley was always a challenge ('I didn't say I can see a crocodile right now, but I definitely saw one once'). They counted sheep out of the windows. They took the pink suitcase for a walk along the train.

'What a nice big brother you have, dear,' said a creaky-voiced old woman, giving Ripley a smile as they queued for the toilet. 'Where's your mummy?'

'They burned her and put her in a pot,' announced Ripley.

The woman decided she didn't need to go to the toilet after all.

For the last hour, Louise let Ripley and Potato share her seat, and read to them from her book in a soft bedtimey voice.

It reminded Max of story time at school. When his mum was pregnant with Ripley she would come in and volunteer with his class, back when Mrs Chauhan was his teacher. She read them that Narnia book, with the witch and the lion and the Turkish Delight. She did all the voices. Mr Tumnus's house got smashed, and no one believed Lucy, and they tied the lion to a stone table; and every time she stopped reading, Max needed – *needed* – to know what happened next. But she always smiled, and made him wait till next time. 'He loves story time, Mrs Kowalski,' Mrs Chauhan would tell her. 'It's the only time of day I've ever seen him sit still.'

Max rested his head against the suitcase and watched as the scenery outside switched from towns and fields to hills and lakes, to green and purple mountains. He stared out, letting it blur; letting his eyes fall closed as Louise's voice mingled with the steady hum of the train, one hand in his pocket wrapped round the furled wings of the porcelain dragon.

*Kriss had been raised as a Dragonslayer all her life. Not one day had gone by since she was four years old without a lesson: in weaponry, in cunning, in the history of the beast.*

*But this was to be the first time she saw one for herself.*

*The elderly keeper led her down the crypt's winding stone staircase. Their way through the dark was lit by torchlight. The tunnel smelled of dust and decay: a forgotten place, rarely visited.*

*'You go alone from here,' said the keeper, handing the torch to Kriss.*

*She unlocked the iron gate, which groaned with age. Once Kriss was inside, she locked it again.*

*'One hour,' the keeper promised. 'I'll come back.'*

*Her slow footfalls on the winding stair died away.*

*Behind her, Kriss heard a low rumble.*

*She spun, her gasp loud in the echoey chamber. It was a huge space, she realized now. A cavern underground, carved into the rock of the mountain.*

*The rumble was coming from before her: a constant rhythmic sound, deep and crackling.*

*It was breathing, she realized. The dragon was breathing.*

*She stepped towards the sound, her heart adding its own quicker thudding beat. Holding the torch ahead of her, she searched the sunless dark.*

*The flickering flame caught something shining in the distance, reflecting the light back. It glowed, then the reflection vanished for a moment into blackness, before returning. She stared at it, trying to fathom what she was seeing: something curved and glistening, a huge golden goblet or a crystalline window, almost as tall as she was.*

*She edged nearer, reaching her hand out to touch it as the reflection vanished once again, then reappeared.*

*An eye.*

*It was an eye, a blinking eye, vast and glistening and suddenly swivelling her way.*

*The rumbling breath stopped, to be replaced by a terrifying roar as the dragon's impossibly gigantic head lifted off the ground beneath her feet and swung towards her.*

*Kriss dropped the torch and ran, desperately ran as fast as she could as she felt hot flames of breath roaring at her back . . .*

'Llandudno Junction is your next station stop, where this train terminates. Change here for services for Snowdonia, Anglesey, Bangor and Pwllheli. Llandudno Junction, all change please.'

Louise closed the book with a sigh.

There was another sigh, from a seat across the carriage; the tall man who had offered to help, who had clearly been listening, and wanted too to know what happened next. He flashed Max a shy smile, as they hurried to gather their bags.

The train slowed, then stopped.

'Llandudno Junction, all change.'

Wales.

They had made it.

## 11

'We're here!' squealed Ripley, the moment her feet hit the platform.

'Nearly,' said Max, explaining, to universal dismay, that there was another train to somewhere else – and then a bus for an hour.

The problem with Wales, he thought, was that it was too far away.

But that was the point. To leave Southend behind. To go so far that no one would think to look for them there.

'Potato!' yelped Ripley, suddenly stopping dead on the stairs as they changed platforms.

She ran back, wailing, knocking irritated passengers aside with the swinging of her empty backpack – but it was too late. The train was slowly moving off, the doors firmly locked. Potato was lost.

The next train journey was nightmarishly slow, and accompanied by sobbing.

The bus was worse.

It took an hour, winding up and down tiny roads, gloomy with the fading of the afternoon light. Heavy-set clouds loomed above the distant line of mountains. As they grew closer, the roads seemed to sink beneath the weight of the sky, dipping into endless valleys. No one else got on the bus with them. No one else got on along the way, as if no one else could possibly want to go where they were going. Thelma spent the whole journey with her hand clamped over her mouth and her eyes shut, groaning at every bend. Ripley pressed her nose against the window and kept sighing, 'Potato would've liked that mountain,' at intervals.

Max didn't care. He felt a thrill running through him with every passing minute. He'd done it, really done it.

The looming sky was already growing dark when they stepped off the bus at a stop beside the road, in, as far as Max could tell, the middle of nowhere.

'Good luck,' said the driver, sounding as if they might need it.

The bus whirred away, leaving silence.

It was savagely cold, with a light rain falling, it seemed, directly into their faces. A wet road stretched before them in either direction, pavement-less. There was nothing to see beyond the circle of light cast by the one street lamp over the bus stop: no people, no houses. Only the mountains: on one side, a sheer clifflike overhang of rock; on the other, a shallower rise of grey-green grass and purple mosses which continued up into the blackening clouds.

'Where's our house, Max?' asked Louise, sounding nervous.

'This way,' said Max optimistically, striding ahead in the direction the bus had brought them and bumping the suitcase behind him.

He held the keys in his other hand, holding tightly to the sleeping dragon to keep himself strong.

After five minutes of walking through the rain along the road, they found a sign:

> You are now entering Nant Glyder
> Please drive carefully

As far as Max could see, it was the same empty road as before – but it was proof. He was where he was meant to be.

'There we go,' he said encouragingly. 'Won't be far now, will it?'

Sure enough, the next bend in the road revealed houses. Not a village exactly. Not shops, not bustle. But shapes in the darkness strung out along the roadside. Telltale squares of orange light cast from windows; parked cars; and bare-branched trees wound about with Christmas lights.

Tŷ Gwyn: the white house. That was what they were looking for. The sort of house Elis Evans's granny would live in –

76

Every single house was painted white.

And none of them had numbers.

Max swallowed hard. He hadn't planned this bit. He thought he'd just get there, and be able to tell.

It was late afternoon and already fully dark. The rain was steady now, heavier and still blowing at them, through clothes, into bones. Max's trainers were soaked through and no longer purest white.

They were running out of houses.

'*Maaaax,*' moaned Ripley.

He picked her up, feeling the pull of his backpack on his shoulders, the drag of the pink suitcase.

Soon, soon, be soon . . .

'Did you say it was for sale?' asked Thelma, pointing.

There was a sign outside the last cottage in the line. A FOR SALE board, on a wooden pole.

'Tŷ Gwyn,' said Louise, reading a roughly painted sign at a rusted wrought-iron gate. 'Is that right?'

Max felt his heart soar.

It had been white once, perhaps, a long time ago. Now it was dingy grey, with brown-green dribbles of mossy damp below one long low window. There was a hedge, overgrown, hiding it almost entirely from the road. Cracked paving slabs marked the way to the front door unevenly.

It did not look lived-in.

It did not look loved.

It was the perfect place to hide: from Nice Jackie, from the social workers who would come calling, from the police.

Tŷ Gwyn, their new home. Max allowed himself to feel proud and excited and a tiny bit clever.

'Quick, go on, quick,' he said in an urgent whisper. 'You lot hide behind the hedge while I get the door open. We're not meant to be here, remember?'

'Hurry up - then,' muttered Thelma. 'Even my flamingos are freezing.'

The front door was of heavy dark wood, cobwebbed about the hinges. Max lifted the biggest key and fumbled it into the lock.

It didn't fit.

'Give it here,' said Thelma crossly, bumping Max out of the way and shining the light from her phone on to the front door.

The key still didn't fit. It wouldn't even go in the lock.

'Let me try,' whispered Louise.

They scuffled over the keys, Thelma huffing.

'This key won't fit that lock,' said Louise.

'Duh,' said Thelma.

Louise shook her head and disappeared along the cracked path and into the murk at the side of the house.

A minute later there was a scrape, and a groan, and the old wooden front door swung open in front of them.

'Hello!' said Louise proudly. 'I was right. The little key opens the door at the back. Come in. I can't find the lights . . .'

Max checked over his shoulder that they were unwatched. Then he followed the others inside.

It smelled. It smelled very badly: of something very old, and possibly dead. As if the cottage had been forgotten entirely.

There were lights, but they didn't work; he could hear Louise flipping switches on and off.

Thelma made sick noises as she thumped from room to room in the dark.

'Is there a dead rat in here?'

'*Nooo!*' wailed Ripley.

'Of course there isn't,' said Louise.

'Probably a dead mouse instead,' said Thelma. 'A family of dead mice. Who were eaten by the rats. If I was a rat, this is totally the sort of house I'd live in.'

'Actually,' said Louise, 'rats tend to go where there are people, so there's a ready supply of food and water. And I don't think there can have been people here for quite a long time.'

Max sniffed, and regretted it. 'Um, Elis said he used to come visit every holidays. But now his nain's gone, no one comes here now.'

So no one would come looking for them. No one would bother them. They'd be safe.

A sudden loud trilling sound split the silence.

It was a phone. A phone, ringing, waiting for an answer, in a house which was meant to be empty.

## 12

'What is it?' yelled Thelma.

'It's just a phone,' hissed Max, following the sound.

Not Louise's mobile, but an ancient-looking phone with a dial, hanging on the wall in the room by the back door.

Max eyed it warily.

They were hiding. They weren't meant to be here. But he could lie, and the ringing was so loud he was worried it would draw more attention to the dark old cottage to ignore it than to answer.

He picked it up gingerly.

'Max! Is that you? Max? It's Elis.'

Max swallowed. 'Uh . . . yeah.'

'Right. So. You took the keys, Max.'

There was a pause.

'I took the keys.'

'Found it all right, then?'

'Yeah. In the end. There's a FOR SALE sign; that helped.'

Another, longer, pause.

'My mum'll be really quite angry if she finds out, Max.'

'Yeah.' He swallowed again. 'You going to tell her?'

'No. No, I don't think so. I try to avoid her getting angry.'

'OK, then.'

'Right.'

'It won't be for long, Elis. Just till my dad comes back.'

'Yes. I see.'

'Could be tomorrow, even.'

'Right.'

'Sorry, Elis,' said Max, meaning it.

'Yes. Bye then.'

The line went dead.

Max hung the phone back on its hook.

'Max,' whispered Louise.

She was standing in the hallway holding a torch, looking at him like a teacher who was about to say how very, very disappointed she was.

'It'll be fine,' said Max firmly.

Course it would. Elis Evans was his mate. It would be fine.

The others had followed Louise, huddling round the only light.

'I don't like it, Max,' mumbled Ripley, clinging to his damp leg.

'None of us like it, Rips,' said Thelma. 'It's disgusting. Max has brought us to a horrible terrible nightmare house, because he's stupid.'

'Shush!' said Louise hotly. 'It's an adventure. We're pretending. It's all make-believe, like a fairy tale, and we've run away to live in the witch's cottage, and –'

The grip on Max's leg grew even tighter.

'Oh! Um . . . not a witch. A . . . a wise old woman,' Louise corrected. 'Who has magical powers of enchantment and has turned the empress's palace into a dingy mouldy old cottage. But it's a palace underneath.'

'In your stupid books maybe,' Thelma snapped. 'This is the real world, Lou-la. It's just a house. And it *smells*. Of *rats*.'

She folded her arms and sat on the floor, a tight ball of grump.

'Why don't we find the bedrooms, hmm?' said Louise, taking Ripley's hand. 'And you can choose the nicest one. And Thelma can have a horrible one, because she's mean.'

They went hunting with the torch, leaving Max and Thelma alone in the darkness.

'I want to go home, Max,' said Thelma.

Max wanted to kick something. He'd done this amazing thing, run them away to a whole new safe place like a pretty incredible superhero – and she didn't even like it.

But Thelma didn't sound angry, like she had with Louise, or shouty, like she usually was with him. She sounded small, and very afraid.

'We will,' said Max, squashing down his anger, and fumbling Dad's mobile from his pocket.

The dim bluish light from the screen lit up Thelma's face, pale and pinched.

'Look. We'll go home. Just – not yet. OK? Not till Dad's back, and it's all sorted. You don't want us to get split up, do you, stuck in some care home?'

'Sounds great,' muttered Thelma, 'if it means I don't have to live with *you*.'

'You want the police to take me away? You want me to disappear too?'

Thelma stared up at him mutely, her eyes wide.

Max swallowed. It did sound bad, now he'd said it out loud.

'It won't happen. So long as we lie low, right? Till Dad's back, we have to hide. It'll be fun, right? Like Louise said. Like a big game of hide and seek.'

Thelma blinked up at him. 'I'm not *Ripley*,' she said crossly. 'I don't like *games*.'

She buried her head in her arms.

That was girls for you. Ten feelings a minute, and nine of them were different kinds of annoyed.

Max left her to it and went exploring.

He'd expected Tŷ Gwyn to be something like Elis Evans's house: soft deep carpets, big squashy sofas and everything matching.

It was not that.

The kitchen had a rusted cooker, and a toaster plugged into a socket that hung from the wall at an alarming angle.

83

The lights still wouldn't turn on.

When Ripley flushed the toilet, the result was an odd clanking sound inside the walls, but no flush. When she turned on the tap to wash her hands, all that came out was the same awful clanking, followed by a sudden splosh of cold brown water.

The living room was stiff and strange under the blue light of the phone: a hard upright sofa and chairs, with neatly folded woollen blankets tucked on the armrests.

Max felt like an intruder. As if there was a ghostlike family from long ago who lived here and had popped out for a hundred years or so.

As if they might sense Max was here, and come back.

'Let's go out,' said Max, suddenly gripped by the fear of it.

No one wanted to.

'I'm *tiiiired*,' moaned Ripley.

'It's horrible in here,' said Thelma. 'But it's more horrible outside.'

'I'm hungry,' said Louise. 'Can we get pizza?'

They couldn't. There weren't any takeaway menus.

No power. No water. And when Max looked properly at the mobile to check it still had a charge, no signal.

No way for Dad to call them and find out where they'd gone.

It was still a great plan. It was still definitely, absolutely, the best plan that Max had made. It just didn't look like it yet.

'We'll go to a shop, get some food in,' he said confidently. 'And candles. Like Louise said. It's an adventure, innit.'

There hadn't been a shop back the other way, so there had to be one if they kept going along the road. There were always shops in places. And people came on holiday here, right? Not in December maybe. But they did sometimes. And where there were people, there'd be shops.

Outside, the rain had eased. The wind had not. It blew through Max's wet jumper like icy hands. They passed the time imagining what they'd have for tea when the magical shop appeared. Chips and gravy. Candyfloss. Apple pie and custard, and cheese and onion crisps.

A bright light appeared up ahead.

The light moved, grew brighter, split into two car headlamps and swept past them at a terrifying speed, spraying them all with road water.

'I think we should go back,' whispered Thelma, sniffing as it began to rain again.

'I think we should've looked at a map,' said Louise in a small voice.

She shone the torch at a sign by the road up ahead.

Llanberis, six miles.

The nearest town. The nearest shop.

There was no way they could walk six more miles; not in the dark and the rain, not with no pavement, and cars flying at them out of nowhere.

It was no good. They'd have to go back. They'd have to go back, and be hungry, and Max would have to admit it.

This wasn't a brilliant plan.

This was a mistake.

Max Kowalski, the earthworm. Half full of hope, half rotten and ruinous, doing what he did best: messing up.

The walk back was worse, now there was no prospect of a warm meal at the end of it.

*I didn't want to run away to Wales*, he should've said to Elis Evans. *It's wet and cold and they don't know about shops. I want to go to Torremolinos, where there's sun and beaches. Amber went last summer. Can I nick the keys to there?*

Every step was pure misery.

At last they began to draw near enough to Nant Glyder to see the square lit windows and twinkling trees.

There were lights on in a low cottage just up ahead, glowing from behind an overgrown hedge.

Max stopped dead, so suddenly that Thelma walked into him.

'Oi!' she said. Then she gasped.

'Max,' whispered Louise.

There was the wrought-iron gate. There was the FOR SALE sign. It was their cottage.

Tŷ Gwyn.

And inside, every single light was on.

# 13

'Who is it, Max? Who's in our house?'

Ripley wrapped herself round Max's leg again.

Max didn't know.

It was the same cottage, no mistake. But the iron gate now hung open, and inside there was warm light pouring from every window. There was even smoke coming from the chimney.

And it wasn't *their* house, was it?

They weren't meant to be there at all. Elis Evans's nain could've decided to come home. Maybe the house had been sold already, and some new family were about to move in.

'Stay here,' Max said thickly – and pointlessly; there was no way his sisters were going to wait quietly to see what was going on.

The back door opened smoothly, on to the sound of voices.

'There now, check that tap. Should be running clear, if you leave it a minute.'

That was a man: a light easy voice laced with a breathy Welsh accent.

'Yeah, all right, I got it.'

A boy, that was.

'Let me do the talking,' Max murmured, feeling a welcome flood of warmth. He set his shoulders back, and squelched past the coats and boots.

There in the old kitchen they stood, quite unsurprised.

'Hello there,' said the man, ducking his head out of one of the kitchen cupboards. 'I'm so sorry I didn't have it all ready for you. Didn't know you were coming, see! She usually calls. Forgetful now, though. You'll know.'

He was older than Dad; short, slim, a bald head with small but jutting ears that made him look faintly elfin. He dusted off his mucky hands, and offered one for Max to shake. 'Bill Bevan. I'm the man who does for Gwyneth.'

Max didn't know what that meant. But he pulled up his sopping wet sleeve, now so soaked it had drooped down to his knees, wiped it on his wet jeans and shook the hand.

'Oh dear, you've had a night of it I see,' said Bill, his face falling.

There was a snort from by the sink.

There was a boy standing there, Max's age but a little taller, running one finger under the now-clear running water from the tap. He had chestnut hair hanging in two wings either side of a narrow face, a high forehead slanting down to a long nose, and heavy glasses in thick dark frames. He was dressed like an Oxfam shop, Max thought: a bobbled purple fleece and strange voluminous trousers of orange-and-green patchwork, with tiny round mirrors sewn into them.

'That's our boy, Tal,' said Bill, giving him a stare.

Tal smiled politely under his gaze, then waited till Bill had turned his back, and pulled a face.

Max pulled one back. He didn't care. He didn't want to be friends anyway.

'So . . . you're family, then?' said Bill, prompting. 'Elis's cousins, is it?'

'Yes,' said Max, going along with it, as the twins and Ripley emerged from behind him, peering warily round the kitchen doorframe. 'I'm Max – and Thelma, Louise . . . Ripley,' he added, as she grew brave enough to tuck her head under his arm and look out.

'You don't look like Elis,' said Tal, slouching by the sink.

'You know Elis?'

Of course he would. Elis Evans came here every summer. He'd never mentioned being friends with this boy, though.

'You don't sound like him either,' said Tal.

'We're the English cousins,' said Louise nervously.

'Well now, that's not your fault, is it?' said Bill kindly.

'We go to a posh school where the school holidays start earlier,' said Thelma, with confidence.

Tal's mouth twitched.

'We're not by ourselves,' said Louise brightly. 'Our dad's just in the . . .'

Her voice fell away. He was not in the shop, because there wasn't one. She looked imploringly at Max.

'Our dad – he's not very well at the moment. He's sick in bed.'

Max hoped fervently that Bill hadn't already gone to see to the bedrooms: the empty beds; the pink suitcase slid underneath one for safekeeping. But he needn't have worried. Bill smiled with the warmest understanding.

'There's a shame now. You give him our best. And you let me know if you need anything; call to the doctor, anything like that, yes?'

Max nodded.

'You staying for Christmas?'

'No way,' said Thelma grimly.

Bill smiled.

'OK, then. You know there's weather coming? The Big Snow. This week, next week, who knows. You keep an eye on the forecast; the road blocks up sometimes. Oh, where's my manners? You won't want to cook tonight, will you? You must come round for dinner. Your dad too, if he's up to it. We're only over the road a way. You'll see it on the map. Coeden Afal. Tonight, yes? Seven o'clock?'

Tal looked sour. But dinner meant food, and there was no way Max could say no.

'All right, you, let's leave these poor people to their holiday.' Bill gave Tal a nod, turning off the tap. 'Like I said, I'm sorry it wasn't all ready for you. I'd have aired it out, if I'd known you were coming. But the heating'll warm through in a little while, and you've the electric on, and the water. Wood burner's lit, and I've left wood for you. Supplies on the table there will keep you going a day or two.'

The Bevans made their way to the front door, with promises to be around if they were needed, and to leave them be if not.

Ripley detached herself at the last minute, suddenly confident, and marched up to Tal.

'Why've your trousers got mirrors on?'

'All the better to see you with,' said Tal, giving her a wolfish smile: all teeth.

He pulled the back door shut behind him with a click.

Ripley's eyes went wide.

'Supplies,' said Thelma breathlessly, hurrying back to the kitchen.

The cardboard box on the table was laden not with candyfloss or apple pie, but with treats just as welcome. A loaf of unsliced bread, wrapped in paper. Bread rolls. Butter, and cheese. Apples, biscuits, crisps. Peanut butter. Jam. Tea. Milk and orange juice. And some sugared rounds in a Tupperware, with 'Welsh cakes' written on a label in biro.

They fell on it standing, too hungry to sit or bother with plates. Max found a long knife, with a worn wooden handle and a blade that was curved by use, and hacked thick slices of bread off the loaf. They spread butter on with spoons. He ate without tasting, swallowing it down just to have something inside him.

'I love Bill Bevan,' said Thelma, her mouth full of Welsh cake.

'I love bread,' said Ripley, reaching greedily for the bread rolls.

'Wait,' said Max, tapping her hand away and folding the rolls into their paper bag. 'We're having dinner, remember? And we need to make this lot last. Save some for tomorrow.'

And the next day, he thought; and after that – who knew?

'We can just ask Bill for some more,' said Thelma. 'Bill won't let us starve, will he? Not lovely Bill.'

'Wait, but – no one was meant to know we were here, Max,' said Louise, suddenly putting her bread down as if it might bite back.

Now Bill Bevan knew all their names.

And so did the wolf boy, Tal.

# 14

At seven o'clock, they went to dinner at the Bevans' house.

It was dark when they came out, the sky ink-black and every mountain in the valley lost to it. The looming peaks of the day had been stolen. The winding path beyond the bridge, vanished. Only the soft *mehhhh* of distant sheep on the slopes gave the place away: Nant Glyder, Snowdonia, North Wales; their perfect hiding place.

That and Thelma with a guidebook, the open page lit by torchlight.

'So we go, er, north-west . . . and then west towards a road called, um . . . Penny Glider.'

Max sighed. 'Calm down, Bear Grylls. Let's just call it "crossing the road and going two doors down".'

The Bevans' house was like their own cottage – as if huge boulders had been piled together and painted white – but this was bigger, on two floors. Outside was a big muddy-wheeled 4 × 4, and a white van, with VALLEY MOUNTAIN CENTRE printed on the side.

'I don't know about this, Max,' whispered Louise, shivering as they walked up the path. 'They already know too much.'

But Max had figured it out. People who were hiding kept the curtains closed, and the lights off. People who belonged: they just got on with it. So of course they were the English cousins. Of course they were meant to be here.

Besides, Bill had been kind, and Max liked him, wanted to be liked back.

'But I'm hungry,' whined Ripley.

There was a smell of food – roast chicken, maybe, something salty and hot anyway – wafting towards them.

'Hansel and Gretel,' said Louise dramatically. 'We're being lured to our doom. I bet that Tal boy is the last person they kidnapped – and he's probably cooking in the oven right now. The next people who come and visit will get Ripley pie and Thelma gravy.'

Ripley squealed, half-terror, half-giggle.

'No one's making me into gravy,' muttered Thelma, marching up and ringing the bell.

But the man who opened the door looked like he genuinely might. He was tall – taller than Dad – with a thick thatch of wavy dark hair and an even thicker beard that grew out from his face in all directions. He filled the whole doorframe: broad shoulders encased in a heavy fleece, thick woollen socks on his massive feet. His sleeves were rolled up to the elbow, and Max could see a swirl of bluish tattoos, faded with age, all up one hairy arm. He glared at them from under heavy eyebrows, and spat out something incomprehensible under his breath.

Ripley squealed again, and hid behind Max.

Thelma took a step back too.

Louise threw Max an 'I told you so' look.

Then Bill appeared behind the giant, all smiles, elbowing him in the ribs to get past.

'Hello! You're here. Come in. Don't mind him, he's only fifty per cent ogre.'

Bill muttered at the giant, slipping from English to Welsh without a beat.

The giant softened, and thrust out a huge hand for Max to shake. 'Oh, right. Hello. Welcome. I'm Michael, Tal's other dad.'

His voice was deep and warm, with a breathy accent that seemed to be built for other vowels and wrapped itself awkwardly round his words.

Max shook the hand warily and followed him inside, toeing off his wet trainers.

The front room was warm like a bath and filled with orangey-yellow light from a wood burner. There was a dog, all legs and long nose, asleep on a big brown cushion next to a pile of chopped wood; Ripley dashed to it at once to stroke its head and rumple its ears. At one end of the room were squashy sofas, and a broad-branched Christmas tree: a real one, filling the room with the scent of pine.

Michael led Max to a table at the other end, set up with chairs and plates waiting for them.

'They didn't cook him at all!' said Ripley, looking up from the dog as Tal walked in.

'Shush,' hissed Max. He gave the boy a curt nod. 'All right, Tal.'

'All right,' said Tal, setting a jug of water on the table.

He was dressed in another pair of those odd baggy trousers, this time with a purple-and-blue woven diamond pattern. Max wished he could take a photo to send to Elis Evans, so they could laugh over it together. *Look Elis, look!* Max would say, and Elis Evans would say, *Yep, that's my mum's bedroom curtains*, and they'd crack up together and only they'd know the joke.

But Elis Evans was already friends with this strange boy, maybe best friends, and thinking about it just made Max feel lonely.

'So – how are you finding our beautiful Snowdonia so far, then?' asked Bill, serving out a steaming dish of chicken in some kind of wet sauce. 'Been out for a walk today?'

Max nodded, trying to wall off the sauce from his mashed potato with a dam of sacrificial peas.

'We went all the way to the post office,' said Ripley proudly.

'And back,' added Louise, in case that didn't sound impressive enough.

They had, too. It turned out Nant Glyder was not entirely shop-less. There was a little village post office, back past the bus stop, and open a confusing three hours a day, four days a week.

Tal raised an eyebrow.

Bill coughed, smiling. 'Reckon we can do a bit better than that, eh? This is a good start,' he said, picking up Thelma's guidebook. 'Lots of options here. Hmm . . . you good walkers, you lot? Think you could manage an easy scramble?'

Max shrugged.

'We've never really been up a mountain,' said Louise.

Tal snorted. 'You've never been up a mountain? Not one?'

'Maybe they're in the right place to conquer their first, eh?' said Bill, a little sharply. He looked at Max. 'You drop by the mountain centre some time, Max,' he said, more gently. 'Michael here'll teach you a thing or two; a few basics, till your father's well enough to take you out himself. There might be a mountain man in you yet.'

Max didn't think there was, to be honest. So far, mountains meant being cold, and lost, and, judging by all the passers-by he'd seen today, wearing a lot of fleeces. But Michael looked up from scooping mash, his piercing eyes under his heavy eyebrows settling on Max assessingly, and he nodded, just once, as if it was agreed.

Tal looked sour as he cut his chicken.

'I want to do the one by our house,' said Thelma, taking the book. She flicked through the pages until she found it: a map, and a black-and-white photograph of a mountain summit. It wasn't pointed in a peak, like a drawing of a mountain. It was a vast, peculiar row of jagged spikes of rock, piercing the sky. 'Why Drag Hour,' she read, her finger on the map.

Tal snorted again.

'Y Ddraig Aur,' said Bill. *Uh Th-rye-g Ire*, with a hard 'th' and a roll of the Rs.

'Y Ddraig Aur,' she repeated carefully after him, under her breath.

'It means "the golden dragon",' explained Bill.

Max put his hand in his pocket and touched the cool nobbled spine of the china dragon keyring.

Louise's eyes lit up.

'I thought the Welsh dragon was red?' said Ripley.

'Different dragon, different mountain.' Bill's eyes twinkled. 'The legend goes like this . . . Wait, you tell it, Mike. You know it best.'

Michael glanced reluctantly up from his mug of tea, then around at the upturned faces at the table. He drew his shoulders up and back, as if drawing himself together. He stroked his beard. Then he spoke, soft and deep, in that strange accent that sounded as if he came from far away and long ago.

'A dragon lives atop the mountain in the Castle of the Winds. In the day, it is stone grey and sleeping, still as rock. But the dragon, like all dragons, loves treasure. Beneath the Castle of the Winds lies a lake of molten gold: treasure beyond price. Every night, in the darkness, the dragon wakes and climbs inside its castle. It bathes in the lake of gold till every scale and wing and claw is covered in it. Y Ddraig Aur – the golden dragon – flies from its castle at sunrise. It brings the morning, blazing across the sky with bright light, rays of reflected gold – until the risen sun burns it all away. The dragon settles back upon the mountaintop, stone grey, sleeping, till night falls again . . .'

Michael let the last words drift away into silence.

Max felt a chill walk his spine.

It was like story time with his mum again: like lions and fauns and Turkish Delight.

But this . . . Was this even a story?

'Is it true?' he asked. 'Is there really a dragon?'

There was hope in the way he asked it. He held his breath.

But Bill laughed. 'Course it's not true. How often do you think we see the sun around here?'

Then the conversation moved on, to rain and waterproofs and the Big Snow to come.

Max looked at his plate, and felt daft. Of course there wasn't a dragon. It was only a story. Real life didn't have magic in it. Real life was Dad being in trouble, and Nice Jackie, and the Reflection Room, and getting down to your last six pounds and seven p. He felt eyes on him and looked up to see Tal staring, boring into his brain and judging him. If you were Ripley, you were allowed to

99

believe in dragons. If you were Max, it just made you weird.

Pudding was apple pie with vanilla ice cream, melting into a pool round the edges. Max scooped out the dry pastry in the middle, chewing fast. He just wanted to leave now.

When they had all finished, Ripley yawned noisily and rested her head on Max's arm.

'Right,' said Max, standing up and tugging Ripley with him. 'You can't go falling asleep here.'

'She snores,' explained Thelma.

'I don't!'

'You do.'

'So do you, T,' said Louise.

'I bet none of you is anything like as loud as this one,' said Bill, nodding at Michael. 'Like a tractor, the minute his head hits the pillow. You can probably hear him over by your place.'

Michael made a low growly noise, and glared from under his bushy eyebrows as he gathered up the pie plates.

'Give your father our best,' said Bill over his shoulder as he followed Michael into the kitchen. 'You come tell me, if you need the doctor out.'

Tal lingered, hanging off the carved wooden post at the bottom of the stairs.

There was a painting in the hallway that Max hadn't noticed on the way in. He recognized it at once: the mountain from the book, the dragon mountain. There were the strange shards of rock, standing up like toppling spears. But in the painting, there was a sheen to them, of reflective gold paint at the tips. If he looked carefully, they seemed to arrange themselves into a new shape: a long neck, a spine, a spiked tail. There were even what seemed to be eyes – narrow slits in the rock, ruby red and clever.

Max stared at it, feeling an odd pull in his gut. His eyes slid from the gold-tipped spikes of rock to the pencilled name of the artist, tucked in the right lower corner.

*Taliesin Bevan.*

'That's you!' Max looked at Tal anew. 'You painted this?'

Tal nodded, casually tucking a wing of hair behind one ear, but obviously pleased. 'Yeah. I do a bit. Did all of these.'

He waved a hand at the hallway and the stairwell. There were small pictures in frames dotted everywhere; a few photographs of the family, but mostly splodgy watercolour landscapes, of forbidding purple-blue skies over green hills.

'This is my favourite, though,' said Tal, nodding at the dragon.

Something about the way Tal's eyes glittered as he spoke made Max brave.

'Do you believe the story?' he asked. 'Do you believe in the golden dragon?'

Tal smiled as if he'd been waiting to be asked. He lowered his voice, glancing round carefully to be certain they weren't overheard.

'I don't just believe in it. I've *seen* it.'

## 15

Max dreamed of dragons.

He was on the mountain, and he wasn't cold, even though a wind was blowing and there was snow falling all around. He was at the very top, standing on shaly chips of grey rock like arrowheads, and before him was the dragon's castle: the Castle of the Winds. It looked like Tal's picture: tipped with gold at every spike, and more dragonish the more you looked.

'Come on, then,' Max shouted at it, bunching a fist. Then dream-Max pulled out a sword, because even in a dream punching a dragon is a bad idea.

But the dragon – he could see it clearly now, the head, the spine, the folded wings – was sleeping soundly.

Max could step past it and into the castle. Into the castle and to the lake of gold. All he had to do was walk.

*Move*, he said to himself. *Move*.

'Move where?' said Ripley crossly.

Her tumbly hair fell into his face and Max woke up with a start. Ripley was kneeling on his bed, glaring at him sleepily.

'You woke me up,' she said sternly.

Max got up, pulled on his damp trainers, and stepped out into the morning.

The eighteenth of December. Seven days till Christmas.

Dark still hung in the valley like damp velvet to the skin.

The dim garden was dew-fresh and cold. Cloud hung in long low beds, almost near enough to touch. Beyond was a field filled with sheep. Beyond that, lost to the dark and the cloud, was the mountain. Y Ddraig Aur: the golden dragon.

Max breathed in. The air was almost too fresh. It smelled so different from home: wet grass and rocks and sheep poo and something else – oxygen, maybe. Air was made out of oxygen. And in the town, Max wondered, perhaps it was used up by chip vans and funfair doughnuts and cars. Out here, in the mountains, there was more than enough to go round.

Here, it smelled of earth, and rock; things growing, and things mouldering. It smelled alive.

Max felt a tingle of something behind the air too. Like electricity. Like a humming of something old and ancient, deep beneath his feet and growing up through the blades of grass and along the branches of trees and finding its way into the rolling cloud up to the hidden sky above.

He felt it thrum up through his bones and into his fingertips –

'Hello! What's your name?'

Ripley's skipping footsteps broke his reverie.

It was a sheep. A black sheep: black-faced and brown-eyed, with thick curls of grey-black wool. With a jolt, Max realized it was not in the field beyond, with the others. It was in the garden, standing under a tree. In their garden. Stepping through the grass towards Max, as if he might be food.

'I shall call you New Potato,' said Ripley. 'You're going to be my best friend.'

She stepped forward fearlessly, and pulled the silver plastic tiara from her head, balancing it awkwardly about the sheep's ears.

*Mehhhh*, said the sheep.

It blinked ruefully at Max.

Then it bolted, twisting its round body through a hidden gap in the fence and returning to the field beyond, the tiara now dangling jauntily off one ear.

Max grinned.

That never happened at home either.


Back inside, the twins were up, eating buttery toast round the kitchen table.

Louise wore huge woollen socks on her feet and a big red fleece, borrowed from the wardrobes in her bedroom.

'This book is amazing,' she gushed, her eyes wide. 'It's got bosoms in it.'

Max could see that; there was a pair of them on the cover, bursting out of a girl's dress while she fell into the arms of a muscular man with flowing long dark hair, and a kilt. It was called *The Scots Bride's Lament*. It didn't look like Louise's usual sort of thing at all – but she kept her eyes glued to the page as she ate.

'Who has a house without a TV?' Thelma moaned as she buttered more toast. 'It's like ye olden days.'

'We'll be all right. Elis Evans used to come here on holiday every year, and he liked it. There's probably loads of stuff to do.'

Thelma rolled her eyes and went to sit on the sofa, facing the now cold, ash-filled wood burner and staring at it in case it magically started picking up Nickelodeon.

All Max wanted to do was go to the Bevans' and talk to Tal. About the painting: about the golden dragon he had seen. But Tal was at school, and the day dragged its heels unkindly.

If he stopped to think, Max's mind filled up with worries. Nice Jackie wanting her suitcase; the police wanting Dad; some social worker with a briefcase wanting to take them away, maybe forever. And having to go back and face it all one day. So he kept busy.

There were two copper cauldrons either side of the wood burner, with some thin sticks of ready-cut kindling and a few logs left. Max took Ripley out and picked more wood from the garden, wet twigs and mossy branches from the rain-tipped grass. There was no sign of the black sheep though; only the plastic tiara, now snagged on a fence in the field beyond. He peered into cupboards hung with coats and waterproofs; at the rack of well-loved walking boots.

He paced the little garden, holding up Dad's mobile phone, hunting for a signal. Two bars, if you stood in just the right spot with your arm in the air. Just enough for Dad to call.

By the time the clock in the kitchen ticked round to three, Max had had enough.

Louise was on her third of the bosomy books: *The Frenchman's Bride*, with another muscular man with flowing hair on the cover (this time wearing a beret and a striped shirt), and more bosoms.

Thelma had found a book called *Welsh for Beginners*, and was lisping and coughing over every word.

Ripley had piled up the charred old sticks and lumps of burnt wood inside the wood burner to 'make a fire', her hands and sleeves and her nose where she'd scratched it now covered in ash and charcoal.

At three, Max tucked Thelma's guidebook into his pocket and slipped out across the road.

It was growing dark again already, and there was a bitter dry cold. Max walked to the end of the lane and sat on the rough stone wall beneath a street lamp, huddling in his squirrel jumper to wait.

He pulled the book from the back of his jeans. It fell open at the right page, as if it knew who was reading it.

*Y Ddraig Aur may not boast the fame and kudos of a 1,000m mountain, but what it lacks in stature it certainly makes up in drama. The rock formations of the summit are popular with photographers, and there's enjoyment for walkers too. Most choose the long, challenging ascent up Crib Ysgafn to the Cantilever. To avoid this long Grade One scramble, the ascent of the south face begins in Glyder, with a deceptively easy winding path giving way to a punishing scree slope and a shorter scramble. From here the picturesque Castle of the Winds lies only footsteps away. The descent through the Devil's Kitchen makes a good morning's circuit for the regular walker.*

Max read it three times.

This was a terrible guidebook. There was nothing about lakes of gold, or dragons. He didn't much fancy the punishing scree, whatever that was.

It couldn't be that hard to climb anyway. People in fleeces did it.

Max peered into the dim grey-green rise behind Tŷ Gwyn. A soft pale line zigzagged up and up in the distance, rising from the black sheep field. That was the deceptively easy winding path, then. But it didn't lead to the top. Mountains didn't go up to a neat point: they rose in clumps and dips, sheer climbs and flat platforms. The jagged rocks of the Castle of the Winds were far above, out of sight. To be seen only if earned.

He could go now, and have a look. He could just have a look.

'You coming in, then?' said an amused voice.

Tal was climbing out of the $4 \times 4$ in the Bevans' drive, wearing a neat green-and-grey school uniform that looked utterly wrong on him, like a spacesuit or a coat of fur.

Max didn't quite manage to walk as slowly as he had meant to up the path.

## 16

The Bevans' house might still have been gingerbread. Welcoming light glowed from the windows, golden and orange and yellow. Coffee smells mixed with twists of woodsmoke, rising from the chimney.

Inside was warm. Max could feel himself gently steaming as Tal led him upstairs, wet trainers left in the hall by the row of boots.

The carpet was deep under his feet, with a pattern of stripes. The walls were crumbly stone, old blocks and plaster, with no paint or paper to cover them up. The house felt old, but not like the Evans's place. Old but alive, like an oak tree.

Tal's room was not like Elis Evans's, with its neat rows of figurines in plastic boxes and all his clothes folded in squares. It wasn't like Max's bedroom either, with its war of flamingos and books and Ripley's latest pet. Tal's room was like a cave. Max felt old hands at work, as in the cottage; a twiggy old witch behind the hairy rough-woven rugs across the wooden floorboards, her eye in the greens and browns and sky-like greys of the blankets heaped upon the bed. No TV, no music.

'Shoo, Tiger,' said Tal, nudging the dog who was snoozing on the bed, her long legs hanging off the edge like sticks.

She shook her ears and padded away, claws clicking on the wood floor.

But Max didn't watch her go: he was too busy staring at the walls. They were the same rough untouched stone of the stairway, but they were strung with colour and life and magic. Picture after picture, in the same swirling style as Tal's dragon by the door. Spiralling blue-purple skies and glittering stars, above looming mountains tipped with pines. Snow-white mornings by a cool unrippled lake. People, too. Strange people, in clothes odder than Tal's own: an old man with a long white beard, his hands reaching to the clouds. And eagles circling above a rocky peak; a ghost-white ship flying through night, leaving a scattering of silver stars in its wake; a young woman with flowing hair, wearing a golden dress, and riding a white horse that seemed to glow off the page.

None were signed, but he knew they were all Tal's. There was something of him in all of them.

No wonder Elis Evans was his friend.

Max felt a pang of envy. They probably painted together, on holidays. They probably did a million things Max couldn't. And he bet Tal never broke things.

Tal, meanwhile, had slipped out to change into his real uniform: floppy orange-yellow trousers and a faded green fleece. He was watching Max looking at his pictures, arms folded, a touch of defensiveness in his stance as if he was waiting for a review or a rejection.

Max felt as if he was on the edge of something. A step away from opening a door. A bridge to cross.

A thing he could get wrong.

And he was Max Kowalski, and if it was a thing he could get wrong, he generally did.

He looked at Tal, and looked at the pictures, and said what was in his heart:

'You're good. I mean, they're good. The pictures. They – they look real. But not,' Max added. 'Like . . . like you must have gone somewhere else to be able to do them.'

It seemed to be right. Tal relaxed at once, and flopped on to the bed.

'Do you paint?' he asked.

Max shook his head. 'I mean . . . at school if they give you a paintbrush, kind of thing. But not cos I want to. Not like this.'

'Don't paint, don't walk up mountains. What do you do?'

It was another bridge to cross.

Max screwed up his brain, wanting to speak the truth again.

He cooked fish fingers. He spent money on trainers when he shouldn't. He ran them away to Wales.

'I get into trouble,' he said.

Tal grinned at that.

'Sweet,' he said.

Max felt his shoulders relax.

Elis Evans was friends with Tal. Max could be his friend too.

He looked back to the walls, drawn by the catch of the light from the sun dipping outside on the painting nearest the small, deep-set window.

It was the dragon again: his dragon, as Max thought of it now; his and Tal's. The same glint of gold at the knuckles of its wings, and the spikes of its tail. The ruby eyes, sly and wise.

Max lifted his hand to it, instinctively, even though he knew he mustn't touch.

'I only saw it the once,' said Tal, speaking softly from the bed.

Max waited.

'I was five, I think. I was just being fostered then; it was before I got adopted. Michael took me up into the mountains all the time. I think he didn't really know what five-year-olds like, so he did what he likes and took me with him. I remember it clearly, though. He was looking at the map. Had it all spread out on the rocks, on his knees, looking down. I was watching the sheep. Even then I knew what sheep were like: slow, dull, munching away. Don't move if they don't have to – but if they do, they hustle. They get loud too. And the sheep – they knew something was up. They munched and munched, and then first one and then the whole lot of them began to run. They were wailing. Frightened, you know?'

Max did know.

'It was this time of year, thereabouts. Still morning, not quite light. Dark low cloud. And then the sun broke through on the crest of Y Ddraig Aur, this big bright orangey-yellow glow, the rocks dark black in front of it. And that's when I saw the rocks move. That's when I saw it.'

He frowned, pushing his glasses up as if it would help him see the memory more clearly. 'It was rock, only it wasn't. Like crocodiles, you know? Like a thing that knows how to hide. It stood up, and arched its back, and raised up its head. The wings were all folded up, like a bird's. The eyes glowed, I remember. I remember putting my hands over my eyes, so it couldn't see me. When I took my hands away, it was gone.'

'No,' breathed Max.

'I know.' Tal looked sad. 'Imagine. Five-year-olds are rubbish. I'd never do that now.'

He glanced at Max, as if making sure Max understood.

Max nodded.

'And that was it. I wanted to stay looking, but the sheep all wandered back up the slope, so I knew it was off somewhere. Or back to sleep perhaps.'

'What did Michael say?'

Tal narrowed his eyes. 'You don't tell adults everything, do you? Like, say . . . if someone was making out they were somebody's cousin, and you knew they weren't.'

Max hesitated.

'No,' he said softly. 'You don't tell adults everything.'

Tal smiled; not wolfish this time, just a smile.

Max smiled back. It felt good knowing that Tal knew his secret. Not so lonely.

'And you haven't been back to look for it?' Max asked.

Tal snorted. 'Course I have. It doesn't just come when it's called.'

He came to join him at the window, looking out.

Tal's bedroom was at the front of the house, looking towards Tŷ Gwyn; towards the mountain. You could see the soft zigzag of the path from here.

'We'll need something to carry the gold in,' said Tal. 'Rope. And a weapon.'

'A weapon. We're going to kill a dragon?'

'Only if we have to. We shouldn't risk it at night. It might wake up, see.'

Max blinked, suddenly wary.

Was this a joke? Was Tal making it all up, and waiting till Max believed, just enough, before laughing at the silly English boy?

But Tal's eyes were clear and honest behind his round glasses.

'Wait for the weather, Michael always says. We'll want a clear day.'

Max looked at Tal's narrow intent face, and felt his heart pick up.

'I finish school on Friday,' said Tal.

'After that, then.'

It wasn't a question. Not if, but when.

And that was that.

There was no need to explain, no need to discuss it. There was just a plan. They'd do it together.

# 17

The next morning felt different.

Today, Max was going up a mountain. His first mountain, with Michael to show him how.

Max pulled on a pair of jeans and a cleanish T-shirt. Then he pulled open one of the stiff old drawers beside the bed, and pulled out a thick brick-red fleece, with a hood and a zip up the front. It was far too large, and he didn't think it was allowed for him to cut the tag out, so he could feel it prickling the back of his neck. But it was warm, and it was what everyone else would be wearing.

In the hallway, he hesitated.

There were his trainers: wrecked now by the rain.

There was the rack of heavy walking boots, left by Elis Evans and his family.

Max picked up his trainers and held them to his chest, feeling their soft squash under his thumbs. He closed his eyes. Then he pushed them deep down in the kitchen bin, under all the other rubbish, and pulled on a pair of proper boots.

Now Max wasn't just a boy learning how to go up a mountain.

He was a hero in waiting. A trainee Dragonslayer. The chosen one.

OK, so he wasn't the seventh son of a seventh son, or a boy with famous parents, or anyone special. He was Max Kowalski, who according to most of the world was the opposite of special, a problem on legs.

But he could change all that. He'd got them this far, to this odd wild place. It was like it was meant to have happened, sort of; like Elis Evans had known somehow this was what he'd needed, and left him those keys on the table.

And now they were going to be rich. Not just for a week or two. Not because of Nice Jackie. For real, and forever.

He'd buy Elis Evans a present, when he'd got the gold.

He'd pay back Nice Jackie: what he owed, and a bit extra to leave them alone.

He'd buy them a new house and Christmas presents.

He'd buy a pair of pure white trainers: new ones. A new phone, a good one. And a GPS tracker for his dad, so he'd always know where he was.

The white mountain-centre van was parked up outside the Bevans' house with the side door open. It was more a minibus, Max saw now; lots of seats, although they were mostly full of bundles of coats, and coils of blue rope with small metal loops attached.

Michael came out, carrying a backpack with another miniature bag hanging off it like a pocket, and a pair of rubbery shoes that looked like part of a wetsuit.

Michael didn't say hello, or ask about his dad. He just nodded to Max, and threw the bag into the back of the van, sliding the door shut with a clang. Then he climbed into the front seat, and started the engine.

Max didn't hesitate. He climbed up into the high passenger seat, and slammed the door.

It was a bench seat, with room for two. Michael didn't wait for him to click his belt in. He just turned the van, paused to check for sheep in the road, and sped off down the valley.

It felt good to be in a car. There were lights and screens and nothing that was ancient or crumbling or mouldering away – although the van definitely had a smell that was not quite dry and not quite fresh. Michael smelled of clean pines and toothpaste, and his hands were broad and strong on the wheel, with a dusting of hair showing at his wrists. He didn't expect Max to chat or know what to say. He just drove, asking nothing.

Max relaxed into his seat, and watched the cold purple mountains slip by at speed from inside the warm familiarity of a machine.

The drive was winding and took them out of the Glyder valley, past the bus stop and out on to a bigger, faster road. The occasional cyclist was toiling up and, each time, Michael slowed for them, keeping a careful berth. But the rest of the trip he took at speed, with the ease of someone in control.

'Snowdon,' said Michael quietly. 'Up on the right there.'

Max craned his head round, ducking to see out of the low window. All Max could see was a long twisting line of sheer slopes and dips, not one mountain but three all gathered together.

As if he could tell, Michael added, 'You'll see the cafe at the top in a moment. Sharp edge against the sky. Row of windows.'

Max spotted it at once: a strange box-like rectangle jutting ever so slightly from the upper slope of one looming black mountain.

Then it was gone, out of sight as they turned a corner.

It didn't look so tough, Snowdon. The guidebook said it was Wales's highest mountain. But it had a cafe. Max reckoned he could hop up there, no trouble.

His dragon mountain would be easy. More like a hill, probably. They could stroll up there whenever they liked – just as soon as he'd figured out the dragon-slaying part.

And he had to wait for the weather, of course.

Climbing from the van, the wind whipped through his thin jeans. There was a new chill in the air, biting. Winter beginning to show its hand.

There was a thrumming, too. A thrill that prickled the back of his neck like old high magic – until it became a tearing, roaring sound.

'There,' said Michael casually, nodding across the valley at a fighter plane approaching at shocking speed, flying low, almost beneath them. 'RAF base on Anglesey, there is.'

The jet ripped past.

A moment later, there was a sudden colossal bang.

'Sonic boom,' Michael explained, matter-of-fact, as if it happened often. 'Come on, now.'

The mountain centre was like a warehouse with a cottage attached. The entrance was a neat low building of white-painted lumps of rock, and VALLEY MOUNTAIN CENTRE painted on the wall in high green capitals. Behind was a modern, corrugated structure two storeys high, with a huge picture of a climber silhouetted against a rocky slope. It was the sort of place Max would've driven past and thought, *Cool, yes, I want to try that.*

And now he was practically working here, carrying the bags in. As if he belonged.

He wouldn't mind making the tea and washing up, not if he could learn a few things. Not if he could be with Michael's quiet competence all day.

Inside, however, the centre was less calm.

It was massive, brightly lit, and echoey, loud even with only a few people in there. Off to one side was a window into a cafe area, with rows of benches and the burnt tang of coffee. The whole of the back wall was taken up with a climbing wall: a steep plasticky series of overhangs and sheer flat faces, studded with brightly coloured handholds and footholds. There were two people on it already, wearing hard hats and light rubbery shoes like Michael's, their bodies strung with ropes.

'Can I have a go?' said Max.

Michael shook his head once. 'Not now. Busy. I can't promise to keep an eye, see. Maybe some time.'

Max thought that perhaps that meant he would be allowed back every day, and didn't mind so much.

'Go on, now, get yourself a bit of breakfast. Olwen'll sort you out.'

Olwen was behind the counter of the cafe. A woman with long hair like wire, an improbable dark red shot through with grey at her forehead like a crown. Her accent left Max blinking, lost, until she laughed and started speaking in English.

'The boy in the trainers? Bill said, I remember. I'll look after you, bach.'

She sat him in the window overlooking the climbing wall, and brought him hot orange tea from a silver urn, and a plate of white toast with butter and jam.

'Don't mind Michael, will you? He's a soft old beast under all that fur.'

She smiled, bustling off to deal with a delivery of new bread.

Of course Max didn't mind Michael.

He watched him all day, as much as he could. He listened in as Michael gave a safety briefing to a group of kids, silent and agog under his strict gaze. He watched as he talked the next group through ropes and knots, harnesses and coloured routes. He lingered as Michael taught a group of women in tight Lycra bottoms to interpret the lines on a map: the grids for distance; the wavy orange lines to show height, and steepness.

It wasn't like school. Here, Max wanted to learn.

In between, Olwen kept him busy carrying empty cups to be washed, and refilling sugar bowls.

Max was stacking steamy hot plates from the dishwasher when Michael beckoned him over, a little after five in the afternoon.

Without a word, he handed Max a pair of climbing shoes, a harness and a pocket of chalk to strap round his waist.

'Come on, then,' he said. 'You've earned it. Time you learned a thing or two.'

Max put on the flexible rubber shoes as quickly as he could.

The climbing wall was tall, much taller once you were at its foot.

Michael got him roped up to a girl named Charlotte at the top. He placed a helmet on Max's head. Then he told him to look for the yellows, and try to climb up on those as far as he could.

The yellows were handholds, small nubby lumps of rubber jutting from the grey of the wall. Some were long and flattish, easy to step on to. Some were tiny bumps, to hang a finger or two on.

Max had watched people all day, struggling to get past the first overhang, losing their grip and swinging free, caught in the safety of the ropes. He wasn't cocky. He knew this wouldn't be easy.

Which was lucky, because it was harder than he'd thought.

Michael stayed with him, quietly issuing instructions. 'Now, try to reach up there, left hand, and pull . . . Use your fingertips, that's it . . . Trust your foot there, Max – good lad . . . Good boy.'

Max fell, twice. His hands ached from the effort of clinging on and holding his whole body up just with his own grip. His legs ached from stretching out, and pushing himself higher.

But when Michael called a halt, with Max almost up to the first overhang, he had a grin on his face and a glow inside.

'*Da iawn*, Max,' said Michael, taking his kit. 'Very good.'

He'd said it to people all day. But all the way home Max buzzed with the feeling of it: of being very good. He pressed his nose to the glass all the way through the valley, peering up at the mountains, now half-lost to the darkness, and whispering, *I could climb that, I could climb that* inside his head.

'You can come again tomorrow,' said Michael, as he pulled up outside the Bevans' house. 'If you like.'

Max nodded.

He jumped down, and began to run down the path – then ran back.

'Thanks, that was brilliant, yeah,' he said all in a rush.

Michael dipped his head, acknowledging.

Max looked up, a movement catching his eye.

Tal was watching through the window upstairs, a soft dark shape framed against the yellow light.

Max waved cheerfully. *I'm a mountain man*, he wanted to shout; *I'm learning.*

Tal raised his hand, just once.

Four days till Friday, and Tal finishing school. Four days for Max to learn. And then they'd climb the mountain, and Max would be rich.

# 18

The next day Max ate breakfast with his nose in the guidebook for Y Ddraig Aur.

Ripley was busy drawing ash-grey sheep in charcoal from the wood burner.

Thelma was reading her Welsh book, and muttering to herself as she sounded out the unfamiliar letters. 'Chhh. Kkcchh. Hhhur. Hhhrrrrrrrr. Hmeh.'

Louise was, unusually, not reading a book.

'I've finished them all,' she said.

'*All?*' asked Max.

There had been half a shelf at least of the bosomy stories; more books than he'd ever read in his life.

'They were only short,' said Louise brightly. 'Anyway, it doesn't matter. I've decided I'm going to write one.'

'About dragons?'

Louise shook her head, smiling with a spark in her eye. 'No. A romance. Just like those ones. It's going to be called *The Welshman's Secret Bride*. Or maybe *The*

*Mountaineer's Passion*,' she said, twirling her writer's fountain pen in her hand.

'Will it be sexy?' asked Thelma, wrinkling her nose.

'A little bit.'

'*Ach-y-fi*,' said Thelma. 'That's Welsh for yuck.'

Louise's face went faintly pink. Her notebook was on the kitchen table, and she leaned over it warily so no one could see.

Max left them to it.

When he got to the Bevans', Tal was there too, in a fleece and walking trousers.

'Taking a group out today,' said Michael. 'Tal reckoned you might learn more if he came along.'

'Nothing to do with wanting a day off school, obviously,' shouted Bill from the porch, wrestling a lively Tiger onto her lead.

Tal smiled innocently.

'He was going to go up Blaidd Ddrwg, but I nudged him to Y Ddraig,' he said quietly. 'You'll need a waterproof and another layer; there's snow higher up. Gear's in the store room at the centre. You can help yourself.'

'But –' said Max.

He didn't know how to explain it; how he wasn't ready yet. How going up the mountain was meant to be something sacred, special.

He didn't have to. Tal dipped his head, checking they weren't overheard, then fixed serious eyes on Max.

'Practice run. Before we go for real.'

Of course. It was perfect: a chance to test out being a hero. You couldn't just jump into dragon-slaying. It needed a bit of rehearsal.

There was a skip in Max's step as he hurried to the minibus, a lightness in the bounce of his heels. A shiver in the air. A thrumming of possibilities; of magic.

He felt a swell of something in his chest all the way to the mountain centre.

Waiting in the car park was a group of older teenage boys: six or seven of them, all kitting up in hats and matching blue waterproofs.

Five minutes later they were back on the road, Max in his borrowed boots with a backpack at his feet, already packed with a lunch and a full water bottle. He and Tal rode on the wide bench seat up at the front beside Michael.

Before long he was sweating in his extra fleece and waterproofs. Tal's were in his bag, ready for when they got there.

Max bunched a fist, wanting to kick. Here's Max Kowalski, who does as he's told and still messes up. Reflection Room Max. Southend Max. It was too familiar, and not of this place; not who he wanted to bring with him. Here among the mountains he was a boy who believed in dragons, and anything was possible.

But he soon forgot about the warmth. The road twisted along the valley and Max gazed out of the window, keeping his head low so he could see the peaks as Michael named them, like a rhyme he was starting to remember: Tryfan, Glyder Fach, Glyder Fawr, Y Garn. The lake, Llyn Ogwen.

The older boys didn't care, though. They were fighting over one mobile phone, laughing at a selfie of the one named Harry with his woolly hat pulled down over his eyes. Max glared at them. Why weren't they looking? Why weren't they saying, *Wow, I've never been anywhere like this, I've never seen all this green and this space – and how soon can I get out in it?* There could be old high magic flowing from the mountaintops, and they'd slide right past it.

'Their loss,' said Michael softly, as if Max had said it out loud.

Max felt noticed, and it felt good.

They parked up beside a smattering of cars, not far from Max's cottage.

The group of boys milled around, fussing with laces.

Max mentally mapped out the path before them: a road at first, giving way to grass and rocky clumps in the distance to carry them on.

He looked up, and up. The peak was out of sight.

With a grumble from the older boys, they struck out. It was easy going at first, the clear path offering steps whenever it grew steeper, and Max and Tal took the lead, Max keen to reach it all first. But after ten minutes he was sweating hard, even with his waterproof now bundled into his backpack. Ahead, the path bore right, round a column of rock, and there they found it: the punishing scree.

It was steep, and unforgiving. A path of sorts had been carved out in another zigzag, but it slipped away underfoot and sent hundreds of tiny rocks scattering behind you with every step. Max's boot kept sinking in and slipping away. It was slow, and painful, every hand he put out to steady himself catching on sharp flinty chips of rock.

'Not far now,' breathed Tal, nodding up at the last few zigzags. 'It's a pig, this path.'

Max bristled. He was struggling: he didn't need it pointing out.

But Tal was breathing hard too, his boots sliding out from under him, his face red. At one point he slipped down onto his hands and knees, crying out.

Max helped him up with a tug of his arm. They were struggling together. At the top of the scree, the path gave way to a flat sheep track through pockets of marsh grass and spongy moss, high up enough now to be crusted with a coating of ice, which cracked satisfyingly under his boots.

Max stopped, suddenly.

There were footprints in the ice.

He glanced at Tal, wary. They weren't alone. Someone else was up here. On his mountain, and getting to the top first.

What if they had come for the dragon? It was an old legend. Other people had to want the gold too.

'Come on,' he murmured, speeding up.

They walked on with a new urgency, climbing steeply up once more.

He could see them now: two bright dots in the far distance: one red coat, one yellow, and he heard a dog barking far off, though it was too small to see. Ahead, but catchable, if they hurried.

'Rest stop,' said Michael, as at last they reached a level section surrounded by ice-tipped grass and mud. 'Five minutes. Drink some water; there's tea in that flask if you want it.'

The boys all threw off their backpacks. They lay in the icy grass. Max stayed on his feet, his eyes on the two bright coats ahead as they began to tackle the rocks above. It was daylight. The dragon would be sleeping; indistinguishable from the rock itself. Hundreds of people had climbed this mountain before him, and none of them had woken the beast. But still Max couldn't bear them beating him to it. Waiting was agony.

After what seemed like an hour, Michael relaced his boots, threw the last of his steaming tea into the grass, and recapped the flask.

'Up now. No need to rest till the top.'

He turned – as the still cold sky was filled with a terrible howl, that came to a sudden, sickening, high-pitched halt.

Max spun, gazing up, searching the rock.

'Did someone fall?' asked Harry.

'That wasn't human,' said Tal quietly.

Max felt a chill run from his gut right up into his throat. It was daylight. It couldn't be – it couldn't possibly be –

'Follow me,' said Michael, his voice clear but urgent. 'Everyone. No noise, no fuss.'

Max stepped in behind Tal and matched him step for step up the gully, over the crest and on to the next rise. The path here was rockier, the stones between the mud slick with ice and treacherous underfoot. Max put his hand down twice to catch himself. His fingers were raw with the cold, but he couldn't stop. They had to get up there, to see, to know.

The wind was picking up, but he made out snatches of voices on the wind: wordless, broken. Then, below, a painful keening noise that clutched at his heart like a fist, so lonely and helpless it was.

Tal stopped so suddenly that Max bumped right into him with a gasp. Then he looked up, and saw why.

Michael was a few metres ahead, his back to them, one hand held up to signal a halt. Before him lay a tragedy. Max's quarry – the red coat and the yellow – were two women, one with greyish wisps of hair, one younger and darker. The older knelt beside the dog: a black-and-white springer spaniel, awkwardly on its side among the sharp rocks. Its mottled chest was pumping hard, and it whined in pain with every rise and fall. Its front legs fought with the air, trying to move, but the back legs simply trembled. Its eyes were wild and afraid, as if it knew.

'She fell,' said the older woman, in a dazed voice. 'She was jumping up here like a bloody gazelle, as per, and – there was ice. I think it was ice. She slipped. Her back. She just –'

Michael put his hand on her hand, and she began to cry.

He reached out with his other, and touched the dog's ears, very gently, crooning softly to it. He let the dog nestle her head into his big palm.

'Good girl,' he said. 'That's it. Good girl.'

The woman held the dog's head too. And, slowly, the whining grew softer, the frantic movements of the forelegs stilled, and the dog went to sleep.

Max couldn't breathe. It was so plain and so immediate: a life, gone.

Tal made a sound beside him, and when Max looked he had tears rolling down his face.

Max looked away, embarrassed. It was sad, obviously. But you didn't cry, just because you were sad. You put your feelings somewhere else, and got on with it. You stepped up.

Michael slowly straightened up and turned round, and Max flinched inside, waiting for Tal to get a tap or a telling-off, in front of his friend and all these strangers. But when he raised his heavy shoulders, Michael was crying too; quite openly, fat tears sliding into his beard.

The two women hugged, weeping. Then Michael wrapped one broad arm round Tal, hugging him tight too as they cried together.

Max stood awkwardly to one side, his arms hanging stiffly, not knowing where to put himself.

'What's her name?' asked Tal, wiping his nose on his sleeve.

'Willow,' said the younger woman sorrowfully.

'Willow,' repeated Tal.

'We'll get her down off the mountain for you,' said Michael. 'Can't leave her here. The boys'll help, won't you?'

Harry and the others nodded warily, shifting from foot to foot.

'Me too,' whispered Max.

But Max stood off to one side as Michael unfurled a tarp and rolled the small body inside it; stayed back as Tal placed three stones upon each other, a marker, a goodbye; walked silently as Michael lifted the dog into his arms and carried it down the mountain in a solemn procession; all the while dry-eyed, and curious, and sad in a way that seemed larger than his body could fit.

# 19

Max and Tal waited in the cafe at the centre. Olwen pressed hot chocolate into Max's hands, but it had a skin on top and he didn't want it. All he could think of was the whining of the dog, and the way its body moved: such fast frantic breaths, then such stillness.

It was death, captured behind his eyes, and he didn't know how to look at anything else the same ever again.

It wasn't a new feeling.

That didn't help.

He felt like crying, but he didn't.

He held his chocolate until it went cold.

He sat still.

'We had a dog before Tiger,' said Tal quietly. 'She was called Seren. She was an Irish wolfhound and she was as big as me. She had missing teeth that made her dribble, and she used to sleep on my bed even though I was meant to make her not. She got a tumour in the end, in her spine. Her back legs just stopped working. So we did the right thing.' He sounded sure as he said it, a well-told phrase, but then he frowned. 'It wasn't like that, though. It was – quick. And sad. But not like that.'

Max held his cup.

Then Michael came back, and knocked the table. 'Come,' he said gruffly, tilting his head to the doors.

The dog and the women were gone, and the group of students were packing up their bags and heading away in a minibus of their own.

Michael drove them home in silence.

'Come in, Max,' said Michael when they arrived; a command more than an offer.

Max nodded dimly and did as he was told.

In the kitchen, Bill was soft-faced and gentle, hugging Tal tightly and crooning to him as Tal let a few more tears come.

'Such a shock,' he said. 'Such a shame. But it was good that you were there, yes? It was good that you could help them.'

Tal nodded into Bill's stomach.

Max stood awkwardly in the kitchen doorway.

'Hug, Max? I don't charge.'

Bill opened out one arm with a smile and a raised eyebrow.

Max shook his head.

'Not a hugger. Fair enough. Cup of tea, then? And something to eat. You need food after a shock like that. Sit down, kids.'

They had strong tea from a pot, and thick slices of claggy carrot cake that Max's tongue disliked but his body wanted. He picked off the icing and picked out the nuts, but the rest went down in a few bites and he liked the way it sat in his middle like a lump of kindness.

Tiger wandered into the kitchen, snuffling at the floor and clicking her claws on the slate.

'Hey, girl,' said Bill, ruffling her head as it rested on his knee. 'You know what's up, don't you? She's a sensitive one, this. Always knows when people need a bit of a wet-nose nudge to help them out.'

Max didn't think that was what he needed; it was too close, and too sad. But he touched the dog's back with a finger when she walked past to nuzzle into Tal's waiting hands, and felt hot hair and muscle, alive and good.

'Take her out, Tal, will you? She's only had a quick nose outside today. Been a busy morning.'

Tal went to fetch the lead and his coat, and Max started to stand up too, but Bill shook his head. 'No, I've a job for you, Max. If that's OK.'

The job was chopping wood in the garden. It meant using an axe – a small one, but real, heavy with a sharp blade – and splitting short thick logs into smaller, quicker-to-burn ones. There was a hefty tree stump, cut flat like a table, and you placed the log upright and swung, and hit it in the centre till it split into two perfect halves.

It did when Bill hit it, at least. He made it look easy, but for Max it was hard. The axe was heavier than it seemed, and instead of coming down neatly in the centre of each log it sometimes glanced off the side, or hit the tree trunk instead. Once or twice it nearly swung all the way into Max's leg.

Max hated the axe, hated the log. But Bill watched with no annoyance, no impatience. He waited until Max was brimful with frustration, till he threw the axe down into the grass still lumpy with melting snow. He left a space for the feelings to be felt. Then he asked Max to pick up the axe again.

'Let me teach you a trick. Can I do that?'

Max didn't want to have to learn. But he wanted to know how to split wood, and he wanted to hold the axe again.

Bill showed Max the secret: to lift and then to let the axe fall, its own weight doing the hard work. Max could feel the difference at once. His shoulder wasn't pushing forward and hurting. His first tries didn't split through the log entirely, even when he struck it in the centre; the axe embedded itself in the wood and needed a firm boot pressed into the log to free it. Then he had to swing again. And again, sometimes four times. But the wood split apart in two clean halves, and the triumph was warm and wonderful.

They took turns: one placing the log on the trunk and gathering the split pieces, one swinging the axe.

Bill showed him how to chip away thin shards, kindling, using careful short strokes of the axe and a twist of the handle.

There was a sweat under Max's collar, and he pulled off his top fleece.

They worked till they had two full baskets of chopped wood.

'We're not done,' said Bill, stretching his back with a groan. 'We'll not want to run out when the Big Snow comes. But I reckon we've earned a cup of tea.'

They didn't sit inside; Bill brought the two steaming mugs outside, with more cake, and set them on a tin tray on the ground while they carried on.

'So how's your dad doing?' asked Bill, casually swinging the axe.

'All right,' said Max.

It didn't seem right, lying to Bill. Not now, when he was teaching him, and feeding him cake. But Max had secrets to keep.

'What's wrong with him, Max? If you don't mind me asking.'

Max lifted another split log from the trunk, and put a new one in place.

'You don't have to answer, if it feels too private now. Just . . . he's been in bed a while. More than a cold, hmm?'

'He does that sometimes,' said Max quietly. 'He just – stops. He – he says it's like a big cloud has caught him up and is pushing him out of sight.'

It came out without him meaning to say it, and it wasn't Dad he was talking about, not big, bright Pete

Kowalski who always had a joke and a smile. It was Mum who had sunk into silences in the middle of dinner and had to go to bed. It was Mum he'd heard crying in the shower and not being able to stop.

And it was wrong to tell Bill, because it was a lie. But it was a truth. Not Dad's. But it belonged to Max.

Bill swung the axe, and chopped the wood.

'I wondered if it might be something like that.'

'The doctor's tried some things. Like, pills. And talking to someone on the phone.' Max caught himself before he said the wrong thing. 'He's tried writing lists of nice things to do. We gave him a sticker chart once. You know? When you get a sticker for brushing your teeth or going to bed when you're told, or not swearing.'

Bill laughed a little at that.

'I know them, yes. So what was on his?'

'Some of the same things. Getting out of bed on time. Leaving the house on time. Washing properly. And then hers –' Max coughed – 'Ripley's had putting toys away on, but his was stuff like playing as well. Like going to the shops, and having a nice dinner. Scheduled fun, she called it. My mum – um . . . she was still around then.'

Bill nodded, not noticing the slip.

'That sounds hard. For him. For you too, I bet.'

Max shrugged, and reached for the axe.

'We do OK.'

He let the axe fall, over and over, Bill removing the split halves and quarters when they reached the right size.

'I had a friend,' said Bill, after a while. 'A girlfriend, who got depressed. It's not the same for everyone. But I saw a little of it. She didn't like getting out of bed either.'

'It was after Ripley was born, I think,' said Max. He chose his words carefully. 'Everyone was so tired. She was poorly a lot; Mum thought she had something wrong with her.'

It felt strange, talking about it. No one talked about it. Not then, except for shouting, and he'd been small, like Ripley, and it had been confusing, and mostly he'd been mad that this red squally baby had come and eaten up his mum. Definitely not now.

'And where is your mum now, Max? If you don't want to tell me, you don't have to.'

'She's in the sea off Southend Pier,' said Max, setting the axe on the next log and not quite having the will to lift it.

Bill raised an eyebrow. 'Oh,' he said. 'Her ashes?'

Max nodded, grateful. 'It was Louise's idea. Mum always liked to look out from there and watch the waves. And the sea goes everywhere, so it's like she's gone on a holiday all round the world. Louise said.'

They were going to scatter them from the top of the cliffs. But the day had been windy, and when his dad unscrewed the urn and opened the bag inside, the ashes began to blow about, up in the air, back upon his jacket like a carpet of dust. His dad had put his hand to it and she was on his fingertips.

So they'd gone to the long-stretched beach, tide out, and walked and walked through boot-sucking sand to the low lap of the sea. Dad had waded in and upended the bag into the water. She swirled round his ankles like froth in a bath. She washed away with blobs of seaweed and bobbing plastic bottle lids. Then a dog came splashing through the water, jumping up, and Dad shooed it away and said, 'Come on then, let's get some dinner down you lot.'

'It was a car,' said Max, answering the question Bill hadn't asked. 'She was crossing the road on the way to the hairdresser's. And there was a car, coming round the corner, and – she died instantly, they said. She didn't, really, though. She died in the ambulance. I was listening when they told Dad. But they didn't tell us that. Instantly, they said.'

Bill said nothing. He didn't try to be kind, or sorry. He just listened.

Max lifted the axe and let it fall.

'Do you think the dog knew what was happening?' asked Max, wresting the axe from the tip of the log and lifting it again.

Bill blinked at the sudden shift in subject, then caught up. He opened his mouth to answer, then hesitated.

'Do you know, Max, it's hard to say. Perhaps the dog knew it was hurt badly; that it was in pain. It sounds like it might have been quite frightened. But it had people there with it, didn't it? It knew it wasn't lost or alone; it knew it was being helped. If it knew enough to feel the hurt, it knew that too.'

Max nodded, and let the axe dangle loosely from his fingers, suddenly feeling its heaviness like an impossible weight. He let it drop to the ground.

'I think I've had enough chopping now,' he said.

'Me too,' said Bill.

## 20

Max and Bill stored the wood in bins, replacing the unchopped logs in the outdoor wood store. The axe came inside with them, along with Max's damp stripped-off fleece and the empty mugs.

When he left, Max was presented with a hefty hessian sack of fresh-cut logs and kindling.

'You've earned them, no fear. You'll be wanting that lot, if you're still here when the Big Snow comes.'

Max went home tired and glad of it. It made it easier not to think about anything but the ache in his bones. But the girls would be home, waiting. He'd found Louise in the dark kitchen last night, sniffling over the silent mobile phone. Ripley had sleepily whispered 'Night night, Daddy,' to him when he put her to bed. They missed him. And Max was all they had.

He summoned up a smile, and swung the bag on to his back like a sack of presents as he approached the dark little cottage.

'Ho ho ho,' he bellowed, slapping his imaginary belly. 'Santa's early! Ho ho – Oh!'

When he pushed the door open, he found the cottage quite transformed.

Inside it was warm, warm like the Bevans' house, and there was a smell of hot oranges and chocolate and something bready and delicious.

'You can't be home. We haven't finished!' yelped Ripley, barrelling into the hallway and pushing him away.

In the living room, Thelma was standing on an armchair, hanging paper snowflakes from the ceiling. Louise was at the window, sticking more to the glass. There was a fire in the wood burner, burning fiercely and kicking out heat, and fresh twists of newspaper in the golden buckets on the hearth. Ripley had drawn snowmen and Santa, gingerbread figures and ribbon-wrapped presents – all eerily in charcoal, like some strange black-and-white Christmas.

In the middle of the room stood the best part.

'Look at the tree!' said Ripley.

'The stick,' muttered Thelma.

'Stop *saying* that,' said Louise.

It was a stick, true enough: a large leafless branch with twiggy offshoots everywhere and growing at an awkward angle, not quite up. But it was hung with lights, and paper lanterns in red and green, and stars of golden paper, and, inexplicably, sheep. It was a stick, but it was most definitely a Christmas tree.

'We didn't know if we should,' said Louise. 'But it's so close to Christmas now. And the post office had decorations on special, and we thought . . . well, we wanted . . .'

They all stared at Max, as if waiting for him to tell them off, or laugh at their efforts, and for a tiny moment Max wondered what Dad, if he was here, would say.

But Max knew what *he* thought.

'It's brilliant,' he said. 'I love it. Good job. *Da iawn.*'

'That means "very good"!' said Thelma.

'Ooh!' said Louise. 'If we're good in Welsh, we're definitely good.'

'I made the sheep,' said Ripley, unnecessarily.

'And look at the fire we made,' said Thelma. 'Bill taught us – well, me and Louise – how to do it.'

'You have to clean out the dead ash first . . .' explained Louise.

'Then put in twists of newspaper for tinder; then small sticks for kindling; then big logs for fuel,' finished Thelma. She didn't mention how patient Bill had been when she couldn't strike the match at first, how he'd waited with them until the kindling caught and they saw a strong blue-orange flame licking the edge of a log.

'And now, dinner is served,' announced Ripley, with an air of importance.

It turned out to be pizza slices and oven chips, with a tin of peas for show.

They ate it on the hearth, in front of the fire and surrounded by twinkling lights.

Girls weren't so bad, Max thought. Even sisters. They were just people, doing their best, like he was.

'It really feels like Christmas now,' said Louise.

'It's not Christmas without Dad,' muttered Thelma. 'Like it's not Christmas without Mum.'

Louise looked stricken.

'I didn't mean – I only thought – it just feels like that time of year. Close. Like . . . we're allowed to get excited.'

Thelma sneered as Louise's eyes filled with tears. 'Woo, yeah. A stick. So festive.'

'Will Santa know how to find us, if we're still here on Christmas Eve?' asked Ripley.

'We won't be,' said Max.

'You know that?' asked Thelma sharply. 'You shouldn't say it if you don't know it.'

Louise blinked at Max through tears, as if she was hanging her heart on his words.

'Trust me. We'll be all sorted.'

Of course they would be. Dad wouldn't leave them to do Christmas alone. He just wouldn't. And when he came back, he'd meet Max the hero, who had scooped up all the gold from the lake, and made them rich. Max knew that, too. This future was unfurling for him like a clear-marked path on a map: Elis Evans having the keys to the cottage; Bill giving them food; Michael teaching him mountains. Tal, and the dragon. It was all meant to be.

For the first time in his life, Max felt like he knew where he was going. He felt right.

This Christmas would be different, but better. Presents everywhere. All of them together. They'd go back to Southend with pocketfuls of gold, and everything would be like it was before, only a hundred times better.

Max sat back in the glow of the fire and reread the guidebook, his hands sore and aching from the axe.

The punishing scree.

The scramble.

The Castle of the Winds, on that unreached peak.

They were real, all of them. He knew them now.

Louise read too, out loud, for Ripley. Thankfully not her own new book, but more of Kriss's story from the Dragonslayer Chronicles. Max wasn't listening, really. He was imagining footstep after footstep up the mountain, like this morning.

He remembered the dog, Willow; her furred chest moving and then so still.

It ached like his hands, and he put the guidebook down.

Louise's voice was soft and lulling, and he found himself drifting into her story, watching the flicker of flame in the wood burner. It was much later in the book now, and Kriss was older: a trained Dragonslayer, sent to defeat a valley dragon.

*The blue-green scales of its body rippled as muscles moved beneath its lizard skin. It paced on all fours towards her down the valley, claws as long as Kriss's arm tearing up the earth. Its tail moved in a sly arc, twining and twisting as if waiting for the moment to strike.*

*But the eyes were the worst. Glowing red slits like the embers of an ancient fire, staring her down. She could sense its anger at being woken. She felt the heat coming off it in waves, as the fire within was stoked, building to unleash a lick of flame that would kill her instantly.*

It was all right, this book, Max thought. Like a film. He could see the pictures in his head.

He shut his eyes, feeling the warmth of the fire as if there was not a comforting blaze in the hearth but a quick-breathing beast, covered in gold-tipped scales.

*Kriss paced, letting her fear radiate out of her along her limbs, as Meriden had taught her.*

*Feel the fear, let it go. Feel the fear, let it go.*

*But being here was more than any lesson could have taught her. This was real, and if she made a mistake now, she would die.*

*The dragon sensed that she was afraid. The lashing of its tail grew quicker, the boiling heat rolling off its skin hotter than ever. The great claws flexed as it drew nearer, tearing lines into the earth like scars.*

*Kriss felt the fear, and could not let it go. But with it still running in her blood she drew her blade and held her ground.*

Max clenched one fist, imagining the old curved kitchen knife in his hand. He tensed every muscle. He readied himself for the fight.

*There was a sudden movement to her right, and Kriss's head snapped round and up to see a tumble of huge rocks falling towards her, dislodged by one perfectly placed swipe of the dragon's tail.*

*She cried out as she leaped to her left, falling, one boulder catching her arm – but the rockfall had been a distraction. The beast was expecting the leap, and was ready for her, its body coiled.*

*She scrambled up, but not quickly enough.*

*One vast paw swiped across her back.*

*Kriss felt a sharp ripping pain as two huge claws sunk into her flesh and tore at it.*

*She fell to her knees in agony.*

*Then she heard a heaving sound, as the dragon drew breath.*

*Its jaws opened.*

*A torrent of flame washed over her, burning the clothes from her skin.*

*The pain was unimaginable.*

*She could smell her hair burning.*

*Then everything went black, and she could feel nothing at all.*

'Is this age-appropriate?' said Thelma, looking up from her Welsh book.

Ripley was staring at Louise with her eyes wide like plates and her hands over her mouth.

'Oh! Um. Probably not, sorry,' said Louise, snapping the book closed. 'I'll think of a different bedtime story for you, Rips. One with, um, puppies. And kittens. And a happy ending.'

She took Ripley off to bed, Thelma following.

The book was left on the hearth, the firelight picking out the gold foil of the dragon's scales on the cover.

Max picked it up, swallowing hard.

They had a problem.

## 21

Max slept badly.

It was now Thursday, which meant Tal would be at school all day, and tomorrow.

Waiting was unbearable.

It was nearly the last day of school back home too. It wasn't like at Pilton Road Primary, where you'd spend half the term drawing snowmen and practising for the play. They'd do lessons. But Mr Brew would wear a Christmas jumper, and maybe he'd let Max put up some tinsel or put out the chairs for assembly.

They wouldn't be missing him.

'It's been ever so peaceful without you, Max,' Mr Brew had said when Max had been off school with his sprained ankle.

They'd like it, his being away.

And then he'd come back, but he'd be rich, and he'd have a story to tell, and they'd all like him then.

Max remembered tearing claws and burning hair, and felt a bit sick.

It was hours till Tal would be back; an eternity.

Max walked down the road to the post office, to stock up on biscuits and bread, potatoes and cheese; to have something to do.

'*White Christmas?*' asked the local paper, with a photo of a man dressed up as a Santa standing next to a sign that said SNOWDON, and pretending to shiver.

The girls were fine, at least.

'*Mochyn cwta*,' said Thelma slowly, sitting by the cold fire. 'Mochhhh-in cooh-ta.'

'What's that?'

'Guinea pig,' she said.

'Very useful,' murmured Louise.

Her pen was flying across the page now, several others already filled with her neat cursive. She stopped when she saw him looking, though, and pressed the notebook closely to her chest.

'Private,' she said sternly. 'I'm an artist at work.'

'Are you writing a sexy part?' asked Ripley, drawing ashy smears on her chin thoughtfully.

'No,' said Louise, flushing.

'That means yes,' said Thelma.

Louise made a huffy squeaking sound, and marched off to work in the kitchen, where her muses could be undisturbed, she said.

Max did the washing-up. He made the beds. He ate some biscuits. He did cheese on toast for lunch, the bread carved with the worn curved kitchen knife. He watched the clock.

At last, it was half past three. Max saw the van drive past, and was on the Bevans' driveway before Tal had even undone his seatbelt.

'Come on up,' said Tal at once, reading the worry radiating off Max.

'So,' said Max, sitting on Tal's bed. 'Problem.'

He pushed the book at Tal.

'Oh. I've read this, I think.' Tal turned it over in his hands, reading the back. 'Yeah. It's all right.'

Max resisted the urge to shout at him, and tugged it from his hands. The book fell open at the right place, as if it knew.

'*Look.*'

Tal read slowly, his finger travelling along under the lines, his lips moving.

Then he sat back, frowning behind his glasses.

'She's not really dead, you know,' he said. 'Kriss. She's fine. I mean, this is the first of seven books; she's probably not going to die on page ninety-six.'

Max felt faintly stupid. But also like he still really, really wanted to shout at Tal.

Tal seemed to pick up on it. He read the passage again.

'Hmm. I see what you mean,' he said eventually. 'Problem.'

'Right.'

'It does seem a bit dangerous. If you don't know it all turns out OK. And . . . well, she does have to go to a

154

special hospital run by witches, and they cover her all over in some magical herbs to cure her wounds. Michael's called out the air ambulance loads of times. But I don't think we could do that.'

'You think?' said Max.

They sat quietly.

Max thought of Willow again. Warm breathing life, suddenly stilled.

'I mean, I'm not scared,' said Max.

'No,' agreed Tal.

'But – I reckon we need a bit more of a plan. Cos if our dragon's asleep, it's all good. But if it wakes up, I don't really fancy being ripped up with claws. Or burned.'

'It is a dragon in a book,' said Tal. 'Not a real one.'

'Yeah. But what are the real ones like?'

Tal tucked his hair behind his ears.

'It looked big,' he said. 'That's all I remember. Big and . . . well . . . beautiful. But not in a nice way.'

Nice was definitely not what Max was expecting.

'My mum reads books,' said Tal softly, his fingertips tracing the dragon's embossed wing on the book cover. 'Not like this, though. True stories. About murders and serial killers and stuff.'

There was a crease in his forehead, his pale eyes intently seeing somewhere else.

The words were a jolt. Not murders and killers; Max didn't care about those. But he'd imagined Tal's mum was gone, like his: gone forever. It had felt like an unspoken connection. Something they both shared, like the dragon, that Elis Evans did not.

'Do you miss her?' asked Max.

'Yeah,' said Tal, without hesitation. 'I love Bill and Michael. It's not hard to love people. So I don't know why she didn't love me. They kept sending me back, when I was little. She had lots of chances to keep me. And she's my mum, so she should've taken them, and I don't understand. But I do miss her. Every day.'

He stroked the dragon's neck.

It should have been uncomfortable, but, with Tal, it was not. He had a steady uncomplicatedness about him; a sense of himself that was not apologetic. As if he was fine as he was, and if you wanted to come along beside him then that was fine too.

Max liked it. He couldn't be it. But it was comforting to be near to; honest, and without expectations.

Max wanted to ask more: about what it was like, being fostered; about care homes and social workers and how long it took. Just to know. Just in case. For Ripley, who did better if you could tell her what to expect. But it felt wrong to even think it. Dad would be back. He'd promised to be back, soon, in a few days, by Christmas, and a man doesn't make promises he can't keep.

'Have you got any armour?' he asked instead.

Tal laughed.

'No. But – hang on. Stay here.'

He disappeared downstairs.

Max could hear him opening drawers, crashing about.

He reappeared clutching a red plastic package in his hands; not a Christmas present, but close enough.

FIRE BLANKET, the package said.

'Look,' said Tal, smiling as he pulled the cover away, shaking out the blanket inside.

It was heavy material, plasticky and something else, with two black tabs hanging from it. Tal looped it round Max's shoulders like a cape, and tied the tabs so it hung loosely from his neck.

Max raised one eyebrow. Dressing up wasn't his thing.

Tal laughed, pulling it back off Max's shoulders. 'OK, maybe we don't need cloaks. But at least we'll be fireproof, right?'

Max went home happy in the cold and the dark.

He had the fire blanket if he needed it, and a knife. He could take one of the copper cauldrons from the fireplace to carry the gold. He was almost ready.

Back at the cottage, Louise and Ripley were sitting on the sofa, white-faced and tearful.

Louise thrust a sheet of flamingo-patterned paper at Max.

*I'VE GONE AND I'M NOT COMING BACK* was written in angry pencil across it.

'Thelma,' said Louise in a shaky voice. 'She's gone.'

## 22

Max read the angry note three times.

'What does it mean, "gone"?'

Louise glared. ' "Gone"! Not here! Run away!'

Ripley sniffled. 'She got all grumpy and cross and there was a bit of a shouty thing.'

Louise knotted her fingers into her ponytail, looking guilty.

'All I said was, it's hardly any time at all until Christmas, and I know we keep saying Dad will be back, but he isn't, and I . . . I said we should buy Christmas presents. Just in case.'

'Which I said was silly, because Santa knows where people are, even if they move house,' said Ripley. 'So Thelma threw a biscuit at me and went to be cross by herself in the bedroom, which nobody minded, because she was being annoying. Only, when I looked to see if she was any less cross, she wasn't there.'

'Just the note.' Louise wiped away a tear.

Max rolled his sore shoulders. 'You've looked everywhere? She's not, like, in the garden?'

Thelma had run away before. She'd been found at the sweet shop on the plaza, sitting on the pavement eating a sherbet dip.

But Louise shook her head, looking bleak.

'She packed a bag, took some walking boots off the rack; all her flamingo things. She's really gone, Max.'

Max checked the house anyway, with the girls following him and telling him they'd already looked there, and there, and there. He checked her room for what was missing. He checked the kitchen, and there was food gone too: bread, and some cheese; crisps and biscuits. And there was money missing from the envelope in the drawer: ten pounds, and some coins.

'She can't get far on that,' he said, trying to sound certain. 'What time did she go?'

Ripley shrugged. Louise looked guilty.

'It might be . . . two hours?' Then she looked defensive. 'We thought she was just being cross!'

'Sure you did,' said Max sourly.

He should make them feel better, should promise they didn't have to worry – but he wanted them to feel guilty. Because this was bad: very bad. Dad going missing was one thing: Thelma was quite another. It was completely dark now; freezing cold too. She could be anywhere. Thumbing down a lift with a nice friendly stranger who turned out to be cruel and murderous. Wandering into a field, thinking it led to a path, and finding herself lost; with no way of finding the way back until light, which was morning – tomorrow, hours away.

'I won't be long, OK?' he said, hastily throwing a few things in a backpack from the cupboard: a torch, a map, some water and chocolate. He pulled on warm gloves and a hat and scarf, as well as a coat; he might be out for a while.

'Stay here,' he said firmly. 'If she comes back, you go to the Bevans' and use their phone to call me, OK? I've got Dad's mobile. There might be a signal, up the road. Leave a message if not. But I'll find her. She's too lazy to have walked far.'

Louise nodded, calm now there was a plan in place.

Ripley gave Max a snotty hug, her breath hot in his ear.

'Don't get lost,' she whispered.

It was bitterly cold already. A little before six, with just a few house lights to mark the way.

Max hesitated at the road, wondering. Left towards the road sign that said six miles to Llanberis. Right towards the post office and the lonely bus stop.

He chose right.

No pavement, no street lights. Max put the torch on, wondering vaguely how long the batteries would last and wishing he'd packed spares. If a car approached, he switched it off, just for the time it took for the bright headlights to show the path then sweep past at speed.

If she'd been trying to hitch a lift, it wouldn't have worked: they wouldn't have seen her.

He tried to think of that as a good thing – even as the next car swept past so fast and steered so far into the turn of the road that it brushed his arm.

'She's fine, she's fine, she's not hurt, she's fine,' he whispered to himself.

But his eyes kept seeing the dog, its fast-breathing body, its frightened eyes.

Max let the cold wind freeze his face, and walked faster.

He'd guessed well.

At the bus stop up ahead, on the other side of the road, he could see a shape: a small human, hunched in an angry ball.

It moved. It hunched even tighter.

But she didn't run. She didn't move, even when he crossed the road carefully, and sat on the freezing ground beside her.

'All right,' said Max.

'Not really,' said Thelma, in a muffled voice. She sounded as if she'd been crying for a long time.

Max wished Louise was there – or Dad, best of all. Dad knew how to make a crying person laugh in a heartbeat. He'd start talking, about any old thing, in a jokey way, laughing until they laughed too, because once you had laughed, the reason for crying grew smaller.

But all Max could think of was questions.

'Where you going, then?'

'Home,' snapped Thelma from inside her coat.

'We are home,' said Max. 'For now, we are.'

*Forever maybe*, he thought. *Once I've got the gold.*

Thelma rounded on him, her glasses foggy with tears, her face in the pale light.

'We're not! Don't say that!' She punched him in the arm. 'We've got a home, and we're going back there for Christmas and Dad will be there and it's all going to be . . . normal!'

Max blinked. 'I never knew you liked normal so much.'

Thelma sniffed.

'You know what I mean,' she said, wrapping her arms tightly round herself. 'I miss it. I miss all my friends. I missed the school play. I missed Christmas jumper day. Now I'm missing the fun bit of the holidays when you just watch TV and eat loads of chocolate. I hate it here!'

'You don't,' said Max.

'I bloody do. You would too if you were stuck there all day with nothing to do. It's all right for you. Not all of us have made little mountain friends who drive us off for treats.'

Max opened his mouth to argue, then closed it again. It was true. He hadn't thought about what they were doing while he was gone; had just been glad to learn and be around Tal, and Michael and Bill. He'd been in training for the dragon.

But Thelma didn't know that.

He could tell her.

He could tell her, and then she'd understand why they had to stay.

But he looked at her face, still streaky with tears, and knew that it wasn't what she needed to hear.

'Sorry,' he said.

'Good,' she said firmly. 'You should be.'

There was a pause, then she punched him on the arm again. But this time it was gentler, with no power behind it; like a peculiar form of hug.

'What do you need?' asked Max.

'Mum.'

Max shut his eyes, and felt the ache of it. Her voice, singing nursery rhymes to Ripley. Her hand round his, squeezing gently while he had his hair cut so he knew she was there, before they gave up on hairdressers and just buzzed his head all over at home. Her absence, in all the spaces where she was not.

'It'll all come out in the wash,' he said.

Thelma shot him a hard fierce look.

'What? That was totally Mum!'

It was what she said when you fell and grazed your knee, or thumped someone, or were just awfully sad for a reason that seemed very big at the time. It always helped.

But it came with her arms around you, her warmth, her voice. Her.

He knew it wasn't the same.

163

'Thelma,' Max said softly.

'Dad, then. I need Dad.'

Max swallowed. He couldn't bring him back either.

'It's not fair, Max,' said Thelma in a low voice. 'I mean, loads of people don't have a mum *and* a dad. No one really minds having just one. But not having any. It's just not fair.'

'You've got me,' said Max quietly.

Thelma wrinkled up her face. 'You're my brother. It's not the same.'

It wasn't. Any more than her being his sister was.

He'd had one job to do: step up, look after the girls. And here they were, at a freezing bus stop in the dark.

'Sorry,' he said again.

'It's not your fault.'

Max thought it might be. It usually was: always, at school; often at home. If he'd been better or quieter or nicer, then perhaps Mum would never have felt sad. Perhaps Dad wouldn't have had to work on the doors at Voodoo nightclub. And there might never have been a Nice Jackie or any boxes of rabbits to run away from.

'There aren't any more buses today, by the way,' Thelma said conversationally. 'I found out when I got here. But I couldn't just go back.'

'No,' said Max, understanding.

'We could now, though.'

'Yeah?'

'Yeah. But . . . Max? It's not OK, all this. Us hiding here. And Dad being – somewhere else.'

Max nodded slowly. It wasn't; even he knew that. It wasn't OK.

She stared into his face. Then she sighed. 'Come on then.'

They walked back slowly, in the dark, the traffic still speeding past alarmingly fast and close. Max kept the torch on, the whole way back.

The cottage was a glowing light spot in the darkness, and Max felt bright relief in his bones as they walked into the warm.

Thelma was wrapped up in two tight hugs that went on and on until she squeaked out a protest.

'I should run away more often.'

'No, you shouldn't,' said Louise grimly, hanging on.

They had hot chocolate to thaw out their cold hands, and Thelma claimed to have walked ten miles away and then changed her mind and been found walking back. Max didn't disagree.

'I wouldn't really leave you all behind, Rips.'

'Course you wouldn't,' said Ripley, arms tight round her middle.

'Max says we're going to go home soon,' said Thelma. 'He's going to call Dad. And we're going to go home.'

Thelma looked at Max. He said nothing, but he didn't look away.

They finished the hot chocolate and went to bed early, tired from all the drama.

Max slept deeply and dreamed of dragons.

In the early hours of morning, when he pulled back the curtain, the dim dark valley was silent and thickly draped in blue-white.

It was snowing.

# 23

He got up silently, pulled on his borrowed boots and a fleece, and grabbed the torch before pulling open the back door.

Snow fell into the hallway, from where it had banked up against the door in the night in a small drift. It was still falling steadily in the darkness: a constant skyful of soft fat flakes clumping together as they fell in the triangle of light cast from inside. The ground was covered in a deep layer, perhaps twenty centimetres.

Max stepped out into the sharp cold, lighting his way.

Snow up to his knees in the garden, deeper by the tree and the fence. He stepped awkwardly, torch beam on the snow, eyes on the phone he waved until he found it, those magic two bars of signal.

He'd promised Thelma. It was the right thing to do. With shaky hands, he pressed the keys and called it: the secret number, the one Dad had begged him not to call.

Straight to voicemail.

'Please, Dad. You have to call me back. Because Thelma . . . and, all of us, we need you. It's nearly Christmas, Dad. And I'm stepping up, but – Just call, will you? Um . . . this is Max.'

Then he told him the address, without explanation, and pressed the red phone button to end the call.

He stood still for a moment with his eyes closed. When he opened them he saw it fully. This was it then: the Big Snow. The beginning of it, at least, for if it kept snowing at this rate, it would double in a few hours. Max's arms were already wearing a thick layer of it. The snow was falling faster than he knew it could, heavy and soundless. There were drifts banked up against the shed and the trees, caught against the wire of the fences in odd, holey patterns. The wooden posts of the fence by the field wore thick stacks of snow like pancakes.

Max couldn't see New Potato. He couldn't see any of the sheep; they must have gone somewhere warm, or sheltered. He was glad of it. Glad of all of it, despite Thelma and the worry and Dad gone so silent. This place. He felt part of landscape that was ancient and wreathed with magic. He felt part of a world where it snowed, and you felt it on your hands and had time to notice. He felt an odd sense of calm, of rightness, that he couldn't remember feeling for a long time.

From inside the house, a phone began to ring.

Max spun and stumbled through the deep snow, falling on his hands and scrabbling through the drifts to reach it.

'Dad? Hello?'

'Oh! No. I'm not Dad, I'm Elis.'

Max let out a breath. Of course not. Dad didn't have this number.

'I can tell it's you, you muppet,' he said.

'I'm just being polite, Max. It's what people do when they phone someone, you know.'

Max almost didn't care that it wasn't Dad. It was so warming to hear Elis Evans, talking in his clipped way, a little bit cross.

It didn't last. Elis Evans had not called for a chat.

'Now don't panic, Max, but also perhaps panic just a little. I'd attempt approximately fifty per cent panic.'

'Elis,' growled Max.

'So there's a bit of a problem about the cottage.'

'What problem?'

'Er . . . my mum found out. And . . . she's not very happy, Max. I'm in quite a lot of trouble. She took away my Christmas presents from under the tree. And one of them was shaped exactly like a telescope.'

'Oh. Sorry, Elis.'

'Thanks. I'm pretty sad about it, even though I think my dad's buying me a remote-control plane, which might well take up a lot of my time anyway.'

'Uh-uh.'

It was no use rushing Elis Evans.

'I didn't tell her, though! I want you to know that, whatever happens. But . . . well, she's just phoned Mr

Bevan who looks after the cottage, to check it was all ready for the snow. You know it's going to snow a lot, right?'

Max didn't say anything. Mr Bevan who looks after the cottage was Bill. Max felt a foul guilty feeling expanding in his chest.

'I expect you do. Anyway . . . well, Mr Bevan who looks after the cottage said it was so lovely having the cousins to stay, and the kids hadn't been any bother, and . . . well, she made him describe them. And she guessed it was you. I can't believe you're still wearing my squirrel jumper.'

Max didn't care about squirrel jumpers. He cared about the wall of trouble that loomed ahead.

'She's quite angry, Max. Really very angry. She wanted to phone the police. Mr Bevan said that it might not be the best time of year to do that, because they do get busy at Christmas, and what with the weather. So she's not doing that. Yet. But . . . Max, she's driving up there now. Right now. She'll be there in about six hours.'

# 24

Six hours.

Just six hours. Maybe less if Bill Bevan came hurrying over, offering help Max didn't want. And it would all be over.

'OK, Elis. Thanks. OK. I'd better go now.'

'Good luck, Max,' said Elis Evans.

And the phone went quiet.

Max stood in the peace of the old cottage and looked out at the snowbound valley, still and silent. He claimed this moment, this one last moment, committing every softened edge and gentled sound to memory, down to the hotness of his freezing ears and the rhythm of the snowfall. This was his. If all else was lost, this was his.

Then he hung up the phone, and set his shoulders.

There was nothing for it.

Wait for the weather was good advice, but he didn't have time for good advice. The snow was only going to get deeper, and time had run out. It was now or never for

Max to meet the dragon of Y Ddraig Aur and steal his gold.

Only then would Elis Evans's mum understand. And Bill and Michael too, and Tal. And Dad. He'd come back with the gold and they'd all see why they'd come, why they'd stayed, and be glad.

They'd understand.

They'd forgive him.

But it had to be now.

Max dressed quickly, pulling on layers so he could strip off if he grew too warm and wrap up again when he stopped for a break before he got too cold. He packed a small backpack with everything he could remember from the day with the dog: the torch from last night, waterproofs, water bottles, bananas and chocolate biscuits. He didn't have a first-aid kit, but he threw in some plasters from a box under the sink. He found there too a small square silvery shape with EMERGENCY BLANKET printed on it and threw that in too. An extra fleece, just in case.

One of the copper cauldrons from beside the fire.

The old curve-bladed knife from the kitchen.

The fire blanket.

He set a hat tightly on his head. Then he added a waterproof coat that only barely zipped up over all his fleeces. Gloves came last.

He should leave a note. A note to explain, like Thelma did. One that would be calm and reassuring and make no one worry.

## Gone for a walk, Max.

It was vague enough to cover his back. And to make it exciting when he returned laden with gold.

He felt a thrill inside at the thought of it: fear and excitement, both at once.

Time to go.

He pulled the door closed as quietly as he could.

Max looked back across the road, to the Bevans' house. The lights were on, a golden glow in the dark. The doors of the mountain-centre van were open, ready for that day's walk.

Michael was taking another school group out today, he knew. Max was invited – or he had been.

He longed to knock on the cottage door. It was Tal's dragon as much as it was Max's. Tal should be here with him.

But now that the Bevans knew his secret, it was impossible. He felt his face burning with shame at what Bill would be thinking of all his talk of Dad in bed, unwell in the head; of Michael's quiet hours of effort. They would hate him now.

Bad Max. Stupid Max. Little Max Kowalski, who couldn't get a thing right.

So he would do it alone. He didn't need anyone else. Dad said you could only trust one person, and that was the face in the mirror.

Max turned to the mountain, and swallowed hard. It was pure dark still. There was nothing but flurries of snow in his torch beam: no zigzag path, no purpled moss. This was madness.

He struck out along the field boundary.

The snow was lying deep in places and his boots sank lower than he expected. Snow found its way under the cuffs of his waterproof trousers, damping his socks. But the rest of him was hot, too hot, and he stopped at the foot of the mountain to peel off two fleeces before zipping the waterproof back on, as quick as he could to keep the falling snow from soaking the rest of him too.

There was a soft low *mehhhh* to his left.

Max looked up, swinging the torch beam, and there was the black sheep, New Potato: wishing him luck or warning him off, Max couldn't tell. It stood still in the middle of the path, hot breath coming out in steamy gusts and its woolly back dusted with snow. It was quivering.

'Go back,' said Max, giving it a push. 'Don't come up here, it's dangerous.'

*Mehhhh*, said New Potato.

Max walked on and the sheep followed for a few steps, as if it was planning to be his companion. Then it stopped, shivered, and began to lick at a frosty clump of green fronds attached to a fence post. When Max walked on, it didn't follow.

Max felt bereft. He'd expected company. And a sheep wasn't Tal, or Elis Evans, but it would be less lonely somehow to have had other eyes on the path.

He carried on, glad to have walked this section once before, grateful for the deep cut of the zigzags. The snow lay less deeply where the wind had blown it up in drifts at the edge of the path. It was falling more softly now, smaller flakes and slower, but the wind was bitter. He felt his cheeks growing ice-cold and was glad of the hat, wishing he'd worn two.

Dawn began to creep into life, a slow-blooming lightness. The sky was pale grey behind the snowfall, the snow bluish and twinkling where the light caught its crystals. Max turned off the torch, but it was too soon. When he tried again, a few minutes later, he could see the path well enough without it.

He stopped again, peeling off another fleece and shoving it into the bag along with the torch. He pulled out a biscuit – gone in one mouthful.

*Got to fuel the engine*, he heard, in Michael's voice.

When he looked up again he could see a shape in the distance, back along the path from where he'd come. It was a person, walking fast, a bright red coat against the snow.

Someone was following him.

# 25

Max pulled his bag on to his back, and picked up the pace.

He couldn't be caught. Not now. Not today, when today was his only chance. This mountain was his, his and Tal's.

He had to get there first.

The path was slippery, snow settled and packed down hard underfoot; slippier still where there was bare rock, laced with ice. Max nearly fell twice in a few footsteps, and told himself to slow down. It would be no use falling and injuring himself.

The wind keened, like a wounded animal.

Max was, he knew, doing something very stupid. He was alone on the mountain, in bad weather. If he did slip and break an arm, or a leg, or even twist an ankle, there was no one to help him. No one knew where he was. Tal might guess, of course. But Tal might not be his friend any more; not when he was here, setting off by himself for gold and glory.

There was that other walker, behind him.

But Max didn't want their help. He couldn't let them catch up. This was his.

He chose his steps carefully, pausing every now and then to look back.

The walker in red was catching up.

It was hard not to feel chased; harder not to hurry. But Max stepped and stepped, following the line of the zigzags cutting a clear dip in the snow until it reached a confusing divide, unremembered. He stopped to check the guidebook. Snow fell on its pages and he scanned it quickly, recognizing the line of a stream cutting across the path above, before he shoved it back into his bag guiltily. He'd dry it out later. He'd hang it over the fire and let it steam.

He was smiling when he looked behind him again, imagining it – but the smile vanished at once.

The walker in red was much closer now.

The walker in red was not just a walker.

The walker in red was running towards him, beaming, blonde curls pouring out from under her cap, and his name called breathlessly on the wind.

Ripley.

'You stopped! Phew. You were going so fast I thought I'd never catch you up.'

'What are you doing out here?'

Max's voice came out strangely, his frozen cheeks stiff and unused to talking.

'Going for a walk. Like you.'

'You can't! It's too far. I'm going a long way, Ripley! All the way to the top.'

Ripley looked up through the lightly falling snow. 'OK. It's not very far.'

It was, Max knew; far beyond the rise above them, further than he'd ever gone before.

'I mean it, Ripley. You can't come. You have to go back.'

But as he said it, he looked into the white blur of the path back to the house and knew it was impossible. He had no idea how she'd managed to get this far by herself. There was no way he could send her back alone.

He'd have to walk back with her.

But if he walked with her, there wouldn't be time for him to climb the mountain.

Max looked down at her hopeful face, and turned away, shouting his frustration into the wind. It wasn't fair. It was never fair. He'd tried so hard to make a good plan, and this wasn't his fault, the snow and her following him and Mrs Evans on her way to ruin it all.

'Sorry,' said Ripley, in a feeble voice.

She looked utterly downcast.

It wasn't her fault either. None of it was.

Max looked at the path, and the path back. He looked at Ripley in her warm red coat, far too big, and her borrowed boots. She was wrapped up just right. He had enough chocolate for two.

It was meant to have been two of them going on this adventure. He was meant to have company.

'You have to not moan, yeah? Even if it's cold and takes a long time. If I let you come, you have to be quiet and sensible and do what I tell you. OK?'

Ripley didn't bother to answer. She just flung her arms round his middle and whooped.

'Yeah, yeah,' he said, peeling her away. 'Save your breath, you. You'll need some puff to get up to the top.'

Ripley pressed her lips together and blew out her cheeks, as if she was storing some up.

Max rolled his eyes even though he was smiling.

She let out her breath with a gusty sigh.

And the two of them set off up the mountain together.

# 26

'Are we really going all the way to the top?' asked Ripley.

'Yes.'

'Is it far?'

'Yes.'

'What's at the top?'

'A dragon.'

'Oh.' There was a long pause. 'Max, a real dragon?'

'Yes, a real dragon.'

'Oh. What do we do if we meet it?'

'Dragon-slaying.'

'Oh.'

Max waited for her to ask how exactly he planned to slay the dragon. He wasn't sure himself, to be honest. But she simply looked thoughtful.

'Do you mind if I don't help? Because I don't think I would be very good at it.'

'Sure.'

'OK. You slay the dragon and I'll watch from behind a tree.'

'There won't be any trees, Ripley. Not up at the top of a mountain.'

It would be bleak and barren, sharp spikes of rock and deep-lying snow.

'Oh. Then I'll just watch.'

Max nodded.

'What do dragons eat?'

'Sheep, mostly.'

'Oh! Poor sheep.'

Ripley sighed, and he could tell she was fretting about New Potato.

'Do they eat people?'

'Only ones who talk too much.'

Ripley sniffed. 'You're just making that up.'

He was. And he didn't mind her chatter; not really. It was good to not be alone in this strange cold place he'd never been before. She believed he could go up to the top, and defeat a dragon when he got there, without question. She believed more than he did.

Max kept walking, up and up and up, repeating the words he'd learned in his head.


The zigzag path ended at the peak you could see from the garden, at a tump that ended in a plateau that was deep in snow.

Max felt panic. He'd been here before, he knew, but it looked utterly unfamiliar. Ahead, there was no path: only a wall of white. The sky was white too, fog hung in the air like a curtain to vanish away the mountain beyond. Max felt a knot in his throat that made it hard to swallow. This was impossible, just impossible. You waited for the weather, otherwise there was no way. There was no mountain to climb. Only endless snow and the guarantee of losing your way.

He made out he was fussing with his gloves, pulling them off and adjusting the fingers. He turned as if to admire the view, and saw the valley lying below clear like a picture on a Christmas card: white-edged cottage roofs, decorated trees, snow still falling softly.

It was not beautiful to him. It was a taunt, the world he couldn't have. It was failure.

'Oooh,' said Ripley softly, behind him.

When Max turned, his lips parted.

The fog had drifted. Where there had been nothing but white, suddenly there was the steeply sloping path up the scree, the route laid out again in the dips of blown snow. It was as if the mountain had heard his heart, and laid itself open for him.

He saw a group toiling up the mountain path across the dip in the ridges, on the next mountain: Blaidd Ddrwg, he remembered from the map.

Michael's school group, here from the mountain centre.

He wasn't so daft then, being out here. Not if Michael thought it was OK.

Max pulled his gloves on, and gave Ripley's shoulder a squeeze.

'Come on,' he said.

The scree was, miraculously, easier this way, with frozen ground packed hard beneath a layer of snow. Instead of stones slipping and sliding underfoot, Max found himself setting his boot hard into the snow, side on, and edging his way up.

Ripley was slower, and he made her walk in front for a time, until that became slower still. Then he made her step where he stepped, into his boot marks cut clear in the snow.

At the top Max stopped. He thought of the dog, trying not to and having to all the same. He looked up. Then he struck out across the plateau.

The snow was deep. Too deep for walking; Max's leg sank in to the knee when he stepped into the obvious dip ahead, and taking a step forward was almost impossible. So he stepped back, pulling his leg from the packed snow with difficulty. Ripley giggled as he fell backwards, and Max found himself laughing too. It was allowed, he reckoned. It was work, this, but it was OK if it was fun too.

He tugged a blackened branch from the banked snow, and used it to feel ahead of them, hunting for the edge of the path. There it was, like a lip on a pavement: a higher edge to walk along, still deep but not impossibly so.

He poled ahead of every step, marking the way, yelping when the branch sank far deeper than he'd expected, to keep them moving. The snow's perfect untouched surface gave way to a ruffled wake, and, when

Max turned back to see how far they'd come, he was disappointed – this was slow going, slower than he'd like – but also pleased. They'd find their way back easily now. He'd left them a breadcrumb trail of footprints.

They forged on. Ripley stepped into Max's footsteps, making little *hup* sounds with every pull.

When they reached the rocks, Max was sweating hard, and he pulled off his gloves again and fumbled in his bag for a biscuit.

This was the scramble, according to the book. He stared up at the rock, remembering what Tal had told him. It was a path without a path; a puzzle for you to solve. No right way up. You just kept going till you got to the top.

'And don't fall off,' he mumbled.

'OK,' said Ripley indistinctly.

Max smiled; she was trying so hard to be good like he'd told her.

'You follow me. You step where I step, yes?'

Ripley nodded solemnly.

Wishing he'd had more time to practise, Max reached out a hand and swung himself up. It was easy going for the first few metres, like a broken staircase. Then he reached his first puzzle: a flat face of rock over a metre high, with two possible paths to take on either side. He could jump up to reach a handhold above and swing himself up the face of the rock, he was pretty sure – but Ripley would never reach.

'Let's try this way,' he mumbled, veering left. 'Stay there a second.'

The choice was good; he could edge along a narrow standing rock and then there was just one awkward moment at full stretch of his legs to make it past the sheer face to his right, and on to another tumbly staircase.

'Come up. This way's good,' he said, beckoning.

Ripley's little legs did not reach where Max's did. She stood on the foothold he'd found and stared up, her eyes wide and afraid.

'OK, OK, don't panic,' Max whispered, to himself as much as to Ripley. 'Go back down.'

Ripley shook her head mutely.

With a groan, Max turned his body round, and awkwardly slid down the sheer face back to where he'd started.

It was awkward here, standing not on his comfortable foothold but off to one side to give Ripley space. He felt the wind pull at his coat and as he turned to look for a foothold he caught a dizzying glimpse of where he was: on tiptoes on a snow-slippery rock, up a mountain so high he could not see the valley, could only see the drop. It was a long way down. And although it was carpeted with white and looked soft as a blanket, he knew it was marked with jagged rocks and sharp edges, the kind that could break a dog's back. The kind that could break him.

'*Mmmm-mwww,*' wailed Ripley, her lips too firmly closed to let his name out, tears brimming in her eyes.

'It's OK,' he said, and he meant it for her, but knew he needed to hear it too. 'You can do it. Look up, Ripley. See? The place you need to go next is right there. Just jump off from your legs and reach up with your hand and you can grab it and pull yourself up. And I'll push from below, so you can't fall. Yeah? I'll hold you.'

Even as he said it, he knew she wouldn't.

She shook her head mutely, the tears falling now and snot blooming out of her nose.

'Hey,' he said. 'I need you to do this, Ripley. Cos if you don't, we'll have to go back down. I can't leave you by yourself. And – and – I have to get to the top. Do you know why?'

Her big blue eyes blinked at him.

Max gripped the rock tightly.

'There's treasure at the top. The dragon guards it. And if I can get it, then we can buy the cottage and live here forever. Buy Christmas presents too.'

'Santa brings Christmas presents,' said Ripley indistinctly.

'He doesn't bring all of them. Sometimes Dad buys them.'

Ripley thought about it.

Max wished he wasn't waiting for her to think while standing on a cliff edge with the wind swirling round him and his fingertips growing numb. But with Ripley you had to be patient.

She wiped her nose on her sleeve, frowning. 'Really, Max? There's really a dragon?'

Max nodded.

For a moment Max thought he'd made a terrible mistake. Maybe she'd want to go back down even more now.

But her teeth sucked on her bottom lip hopefully, and she gazed up at him, and he knew she was in.

'OK,' she said. 'But you need to push quite hard on my bottom, because if I fall off I'll be cross. And dead.'

'Deal,' said Max.

It was not as simple as he'd imagined, to get Ripley to leap up a rock and push her from below, and it was not the only moment of the scramble that led to tears and backtracking. Twice Max found himself at a dead end of impossible sheer rock, and had to pick his way backwards round Ripley to find a new path. Twice he realized the leap up was one he could have made alone, but not one she could manage. It was desperately slow going, and with every step he could feel cold seeping into his bones.

But it came with something else too. An inner fire of hope. A sense of purpose, and pride in it. He was getting there. Every step was getting there. He – Max Kowalski, of all people! – was headed for victory.

Elis Evans would be proud to be his friend. Mr Brew wouldn't send him to the Reflection Room. Dad – Dad would come back to see . . . because who could stay away?

The last rocks of the scramble were laid out as neatly as a staircase and Max stepped up them with barely a hand to the ground.

The wind nearly took him straight back down.

Out of the shelter of the mountain, on this high plateau, the wind was free to gust and sweep, swirling snow wildly round his head. Buffeted, Max dropped to one knee, bowing his head against the onslaught. His face was whipped raw, his hands bright red. He pulled on gloves, even though they were damp, and pulled his hood up.

Ripley followed a moment later, and he held out a hand to catch her; she was so small he was afraid a big gust would lift her right off the mountain.

This was no place to be.

It was exactly where a dragon would live.

Max turned his face into the wind and looked into the spiky heart of the dragon's castle.

# 27

It was just as it was in Tal's painting – and nothing like it at all.

The looming spikes of rock were tipped, not with gold, but with snow, nestled deep into the crevices and swept into drift lines along the sharp edges. It was as vast and intimidating as the painting suggested – but what Tal had not shown was the world around it: the towering spikes of rock beyond, as the crest of the ridge continued and dipped before peaking again in the misty distance; the high peak behind completely thick with banked snow; the looming skies so vast above, swirling white and threatening to topple him over if he looked too long.

Ripley's hand tightened on his glove.

Max squeezed her hand firmly, and threw her a grin.

This was where he was meant to be. Everything had led him here: the keys from Elis Evans's bedroom, and Kriss's story from Louise's book, and Michael's quiet voice telling the tale of the golden dragon. His hours at the mountain centre. All his hard work. He had earned this moment.

With care, he swung the backpack off his back and, resting against a rock to shelter it from the wind, pulled it open. The bulk of the copper bucket glowed inside. It was chill to the touch even through his gloves, and as awkward to get out of the bag as it had been to get in, but he pulled it out anyway.

Inside was the kitchen knife.

Then he tugged the fire blanket free and, with difficulty, fighting the wind, tied it round his neck.

Ripley regarded him with a quizzical crinkle of her nose.

'Trust me,' said Max.

He tucked the cauldron under one arm, the knife gripped in his other hand, and stood, his fireproof cloak billowing.

The beast was ahead to his left.

He looked across to the snowbound mountain beyond, spotting the distant blue dots of Michael's group toiling up Blaidd Ddrwg, making slow but steady progress.

They might cut across to this peak, along the ridge once they were higher. They might catch him up.

It had to be now. Now.

'Stay here,' said Max. He should keep Ripley safe; there was no sense risking her going any further. And he should go alone. The warrior, alone.

She clung on to his elbow, shaking her head. 'Please. Don't want to be by myself.'

'Do as you're told,' he said, shaking her off. 'By those rocks, now.'

She made a mournful squeak, and skittered across the snow, half-blown there, to huddle in the rock.

He felt a moment's guilt. She looked so frightened. But she was safer there.

He turned his shoulders into the wind and stepped towards the snow-tipped spiked rocks of the dragon's lair.

The bitter wind stung his eyes. It was hard to see, hard to keep stepping. The bulk of the cauldron under his arm felt heavy and unwieldy. The fire blanket caught the wind and tugged him off course. But he kept moving. The beast was there, right there: an unmoving sleeping form hidden among the slanted rocks.

Max stepped so close it was as if he was in Tal's painting in the Bevans' hallway. There it was, that vast and terrible spine. There were the folded wings. There was the low-lying line of a spiked and evil tail. There was the long neck, and the sleek flat head.

Max stood still and silent, waiting for the emerald bright eyes to flick into horrifying life.

The wind quieted.

The dragon stayed sleeping.

Summoning up every brave thought he could muster, Max took a step forward. Holding the knife before him, he whispered to himself.

'Feel the fear, let it go. Feel the fear, let it go.'

He could feel Ripley's eyes on him.

Max risked stepping closer. And closer. Close enough to be torn apart if the great claws swiped at his heart. Close enough to be burned to a cinder if the great and terrible jaws roared into flaming life. Close enough to touch.

Max reached out one ungloved hand to the low flat head.

It was rock.

Just rock.

It didn't even look like a head, now he was closer. The spine of the beast was just an unusual line of rocks, jutting upwards at an odd angle. There were similar rocks all around.

There was no dragon.

There was no lake of gold.

This was not a magical story, and he was not going home a hero who had saved them all.

It was a clear thought, quite calm. A fact. A simple inevitable fact.

But once he had thought it, it was as if it tore away something inside him that had been in place for a long time, holding him together: a strip of human sticky-tape that had lost its stick at last.

Max opened his mouth and a sound came out. A deep low sound like a terrible song of misery and despair, a wail from the past. His eyes were full of tears that he couldn't stop. They flowed out of him. He wiped his face but they kept coming. Ripley stared at him, but they kept coming.

And Max could hear the familiar voice, telling him to stop; telling him what a man was. Boys don't cry. Stop sniffing like a girl. Man up, big man. Pull yourself together. You've got to look after them, Max. Look after the girls. Because he was different from them, more special and less at the same time. Strong and silent. Daft as a brush but never weak, never needy. A big brave boy.

And – that wasn't fair, either. In all his life, nothing had been fair, but nothing more so than this.

Max fought back.

He was eleven years old and he was allowed to feel, to care, to cry at sorrow. He was allowed to walk away from a fight. He was allowed to not be the man of the house . . . Because that wasn't his job. That was his *dad's* job. And Max had been doing it for him – they all had – and it wasn't fair. It wasn't right.

His dad wasn't fair. His dad wasn't right.

An image swirled through the snow before his wet eyes: a shape, the shape of a man. As if he was coming back at last, just like Max had longed for.

Max gripped the handle of the knife and roared as he ran forward, the blade lifted to strike.

There was no dragon to slay. But he had something bigger to defeat.

He swung at nothing. There was no man.

But there was a sound around him suddenly: not one single noise but a vibration in the air as if voices from deep within the mountain were stirring. As if he had woken something.

He stopped still, searching through the whirling snow.

He could hear Ripley calling his name, indistinct in the wind, as something rippled through the world like a universal cry.

Then there was a roaring, and the rocks began to move.

# 28

Max had dropped the knife in the snow and he fell to his knees, searching desperately, as all around the ground seemed to quake and shift under the claws of the waking dragon.

Its great back was moving, shaking snow from the tips of its sharp-ridged spine.

Max scrabbled desperately, the snow coming up in clumps, until he saw it: a flash of silver. His knife.

He gripped it, jumping up, reaching his arm out to catch her as Ripley ran towards him, her face white.

But there were no emerald eyes or snarling jaws before him, no spiny dragon raising its head to strike.

The roaring grew louder and then, with a blur and a quake in the valley below, two jet fighters flew past at impossible speed.

There was a gigantic bang, that echoed off the sheer faces of the rocks around him and rang through the valley.

The rocks fell still.

The dragon – the not-dragon – was not roaring to life.

It was the fighters from down the valley, not a monster. There was nothing to fear.

Until Max heard a great low groan from far behind him, and spun round.

The high mountain pass beyond was still deep in its cap of snow. But, as he watched, a crack began to form across the smooth white surface of the deep-packed frozen snow atop Blaidd Ddrwg. It rang out loud across the plateau, a tearing sound as the crack widened and grew. With a vast and terrible creak, the block of snow and ice detached itself from its home, and after a breathless pause, as if it was waiting to gain confidence, it began to slide.

'No . . .' breathed Max.

It moved so swiftly once it had begun that there was no stopping it. It crashed a path through rock and ice, pulling with it great plumes of dashed snow and flying rocks, and battering its way down the mountain. It was followed by another slide, this time of scree and rock, treacherous slivers of slaty stone and heavy slabs that crashed and boomed.

Towards the walkers.

Towards Michael, and his mountain-centre walkers.

Who would have no idea what was heading their way until it was upon them; nowhere to run to escape its thundering path.

And no one would know.

'Max,' wailed Ripley, looking round in panic.

'We're OK,' he whispered, hoping it was true.

No icy bank of snow was hanging over them, no tumbling rock. The lifeless stone dragon stayed where it was.

But the others . . . the others would not be OK.

Max fumbled in his pocket for the mobile phone. He remembered a poster in the mountain centre: *Call Mountain Rescue.* You just dialled 999, and asked them to come. Told them where and what had happened. Got help.

It didn't matter how much trouble Max would be in. He was in it, already. It didn't matter. He could do something to help. Had to.

But the mobile phone's faint glowing screen showed the familiar picture.

No signal.

Even here, high up in the mountains.

He waved it around a little, stomping across the plateau to hunt down a bar, just one – but there was still nothing.

'We need to go back down,' he said, pulling off the fire blanket and shoving it along with the knife and the cauldron awkwardly back inside the backpack. 'There's people on that mountain, Ripley. They need us to call them some help.'

She pouted. 'But we have to get to the top.'

'We did.' He looked around them. 'We're here.'

'Oh. OK.' She looked around too. 'I thought you'd be happy, when you got to the top.'

Max followed her gaze, taking a last look at the spine of rock.

His dragon.

Now slain.

'Me too,' he said.

Then he struck out for the scramble.

It was worse going back down, with the looming view of the drop unavoidable, and a sense of panic in his blood at the thought of Michael and the others, and deep snow upon them. They had to hurry, and they had to go slow; be swift, be safe. He took each downward step of the scramble backwards, facing the rock and wishing he'd left a marker behind him to know how he'd come up.

Ripley, meanwhile, seemed quite cheerful about it all, and followed him without complaint.

She stepped where he stepped. She held on where he held on. She reached the bottom of the scramble a moment after he did, and dusted the snow off her hands.

'I quite like that bit,' she said.

'Hmm,' said Max, who did not, and would not, perhaps, ever.

He waved the phone. Still nothing. But he could keep it in his hand now, and from here he could see the path of sorts they'd carved. Their footprints had drifted and were half-filled with snow or blown away entirely, but they were visible, and this would be easier going down than up.

Max walked and waited, walked and waited, a choked feeling in his throat, until at last the screen showed a sudden two then three bars.

The call took only seconds. They wanted his name, and the time it had happened, and a map reference, and Max wished he had a watch, wished he'd known to think, wished he could say the name of the mountains properly – but he told them of the walkers and they thanked him. They said they would do their best.

They crossed the long stretch of snow and the scree and were halfway along the zigzag before they heard it: the slow *whup-whup-whirr* of the helicopter.

'*Nooo*,' mumbled Ripley, clinging on to his arm. 'What if it makes things fall on us?'

But the helicopter was not loud or echoing enough to risk that, and by now they were deep into the valley, more sheltered and in lighter snow banks.

'We're fine. Come on.'

He gave her a biscuit to keep her going. He had one too. He had started to feel oddly light all over, as if the slow thawing of his face and the lifting of the need to slay dragons were changing him. They walked on down the zigzag, and watched as the helicopter hovered, lingered, dipped out of sight in the cleft of the valley, then wheeled up and away, the whip of its blades fading away to silence.

Max could see the road clearly now. The houses. The lights in the windows.

They reached flatter ground, and walked on, hurrying.

The mountain-centre van was outside the Bevans' house.

Max wanted to knock on the door and tell them. The helicopter was out. They should wait for news. And he was sorry about all the rest too, but the helicopter was called.

But there was a car outside Max's house too.

A blue 4 × 4, with the lights on.

They switched off as he and Ripley approached, and the door swung open.

Elis Evans's mum stepped out in her wellies, and Max knew by a glance at the set of her shoulders that he needn't worry about being swept into a bosomy hug.

'Max Kowalski, how dare you!' she shouted.

Her eyes were glinting as she stomped through the snow towards him, jabbing at him with her keys.

'Theft, that's what it is! Theft, and fraud, and . . . and . . . very wrong behaviour! You – you –'

'Very sorry, Mrs Evans,' Max mumbled, as Ripley hid behind him, her little hands gripping his hips.

'Sorry's not going to cut it this time, young man,' shouted Mrs Evans.

But Max had stopped listening.

The other door of the car had swung open.

A man stepped out into the drift, and slammed the door.

Dad.

# 29

'Daddy!' yelled Ripley, sprinting out from behind Max and slithering awkwardly through the snow to fling herself at him.

'Princess,' grunted Dad, as she hit him at speed.

He swept her up. Gave her a twirl.

She clung round his neck like a baby monkey, suddenly not the brave child who could climb mountains, but the family's youngest again.

Dad kept hold, and looked at Max. He gave Max a short nod, like a hello.

'Max.'

Max held himself stiff and still.

'Well, come on then, no good us standing around freezing to death, is it?' said Mrs Evans, an odd look on her face as she glanced from Max to his father and back again. Her voice had a softer edge to it now. 'Come on. Let's see what you've done to the poor place, you horror.'

She stepped awkwardly through the deep snow on the pavement, and pushed the iron gate hard against the drift behind it. She made her way round the back of the house. Max followed dumbly in her deep footprints, Dad carrying Ripley to bring up the rear.

He was in trainers, Max saw. Trainers and jeans, wet to the knee.

'At least you've not burned it down,' mumbled Mrs Evans, standing back to survey the cottage, as if Max might have knocked down a wall or two while he was here.

Max pushed open the back door meekly.

Thelma and Louise were waiting in the hallway.

'Max? Are you – oh! Oh!'

There was a clatter, as Louise dropped her pen on the stone floor. Her face was streaked with panicky tears.

Thelma was beside her, not crying but quivering all over.

' "Gone for a walk"!' she said in a shuddery voice.

She was holding Max's note, now crumpled in her hand.

They had worried, like Max had worried when Thelma had run away. Max knew how it felt. But then he saw their faces change as they saw who was behind him, and it was unimportant.

Thelma's mouth dropped wide open.

Louise made a very high squeaking sound.

'Daddy,' announced Ripley, quite unnecessarily, still clinging as if to make it clear he was hers.

Dad stepped in behind Max.

'Angels,' he said. 'How I've missed my angels. Come here, girls.'

He held out his free arm, and Louise buried her face in his belly.

Thelma hesitated. Then she wrapped her arms round him too.

'Oh, don't mind me, it's only my house,' muttered Mrs Evans, sliding round the side of them.

She caught Max's eye, standing stiffly in the corner.

'Come on, Max. Let's put the kettle on, shall we? I for one need a cup of tea.'

Max followed her reluctantly.

'Sorry,' he said, as she boiled the water and put out the cups, tutting at their washing-up skills.

'I should think so.'

'Elis didn't know. It's not his fault. He didn't know any of it.'

'Hmm,' said Mrs Evans.

When they carried the cups through, his family were sitting on the sofa, nattering away.

'I can speak Welsh now,' said Thelma. 'Not all of it, because I only just started. And I still can't make the letter where you just sort of spit at people. But I know all the words for animals and food and directions and I can say the names of mountains and . . . I'm dead good at it. Even though it's disgusting here and smells of rats.'

'Charming,' said Mrs Evans.

'I'm writing a book,' said Louise. 'You can't read it, because it isn't finished and I'm not sure it's the sort of book you'd like, really. But I've written one hundred and two pages. We don't even mind that there isn't a telly.'

'We do,' said Thelma. 'Not having a TV is the absolute worst. You should fix that,' she added, for Mrs Evans's benefit.

'Noted,' she said drily.

'But . . . well, we've done other things. We learned how to light fires.'

'We made a beautiful Christmas tree,' said Ripley.

Thelma rolled her eyes, muttering 'stick' under her breath.

'We cooked for ourselves, and did the shopping (the Bevans helped a lot – don't be cross because we lied to them a bit to make them help, we'll say we're very sorry), and kept the cottage very clean and tidy, mostly.'

'Bill Bevan said it's good for people to live in it, especially in winter,' said Thelma, looking at Mrs Evans. 'Keep the fire going, and notice any problems.'

'Don't talk to me about Bill Bevan,' muttered Mrs Evans. 'He should have rung me straight away.'

Max shut his eyes, thinking of Michael; of Bill and Tal, and the police knocking at the door.

'Well, I'm impressed, I have to say,' said Dad, slapping his thighs. 'Knew you weren't daft. Didn't expect all this, but . . . well, it's terrible, obviously, very wrong, to steal the keys like that,' he added as Mrs Evans gave him a glare. 'You're in a lot of trouble, all of you. But you've looked after yourselves. You're a right little team.'

'Max did most of it,' murmured Ripley.

Max opened his eyes again. He was standing in the doorway, the nearest place to escape, and his heart felt full and empty both at once.

Here was Dad, back; all he had ever wanted.

Here was Dad, acting as if it was all just nothing. As if he'd been to the shops for a bit longer than he'd said, but he was back now.

'It's not OK,' Max mumbled, his voice thick.

'What's that?' Dad's eyes were sharp. 'Speak up if you're speaking.'

'It's not OK,' said Max, clearer now. 'You can't just come back like it's OK. It's not OK.'

And he turned and fled as he felt his face grow hot – out, out into the back garden and into the quiet blanketing peace of the snow.

He looked up and up at his mountain. At the bleakness of it, the danger.

At the thick drifts, not soft now but savage, more than he had ever imagined.

At the dragon that wasn't.

A soft *mehhhh*-ing called him back.

New Potato was in the garden again, standing crossly beside a snow-packed bush. It stared at Max: warm brown eyes and white-dusted wool.

It must be a nice life, Max thought, just standing in a field with no one asking anything of you ever, and never being wrong, and never feeling like the world was ending. He could be a sheep. 'Want to swap?' he whispered.

'Talking to yourself?'

It was Dad.

'No,' Max said defensively. He dipped his head, shuffling his shoulders. 'I was talking to a sheep.'

It sounded stupid. Dad laughed at him.

Max kicked the snow.

'So I hear you took a six-year-old up a mountain in this lovely weather we're having.'

Max kept his fists bunched up tightly in his pockets.

'She took herself.'

That sounded stupid too. He should've brought her back. He should have left the dragon. People mattered more than dragons, and treasure; even if there had been a real dragon, and real treasure. People like Ripley. People like Michael.

He'd been bad, again. Made a bad decision, again. But he wasn't the only one.

'You didn't step up, Dad.'

He said it quietly, as if it was to himself. But it wasn't.

Max turned round and faced his father; said it again, louder. 'You didn't step up. You told me to step up. Look after them. Look after everything. I had to. Because you didn't step up.'

'Hey now, calm down.' Dad grinned, his eyes twinkling as he shrugged his shoulders: Big Pete Kowalski, who everyone liked. 'It didn't go how I meant, right? You're not daft, son, you know how it goes. I did a few extra jobs for Nice Jackie and – it got serious, mate.'

Max thought of the pink suitcase hidden under the bed inside, and felt sick.

'No kidding.'

'They'd have arrested me right there and then, if I'd stayed. Couldn't have that, could we? So I went to lie low, just a couple of days, and it went on a little bit longer than I thought it would. And then Nice Jackie calls, tells me she's been round yours again and you've gone missing. Furious, she was. So I came back, yeah? For you. To sort it.'

Max felt sicker.

'That's why you came back. Because Nice Jackie told you to.'

Because Nice Jackie wanted her money back.

'Hey! I was beside myself over you kids. Especially when I find out you're up here, because Rhian Evans is banging the door down to tear off a strip off me. She drove me up here giving me earfuls the whole way. She's got a tongue on her, that one, I'd forgotten.'

He chuckled, like Max might join in with a matey giggle.

Like he could laugh it away.

Max felt that knot in his throat again, the one that needed to be pushed down and away or he'd cry.

He didn't push it away.

'You shouldn't have left us,' he said thickly.

Dad swallowed. He looked away as tears began to roll down Max's cheeks, embarrassed.

'You shouldn't have put it all on me.'

'Hey. Hey, Max, I'm sorry. I didn't say that yet, did I? I'm sorry, Max. I got in a corner and I had choices and I made all the bad ones, OK? Nothing but bad ones.'

Dad stepped closer through the snow and Max flung out a hand, pushing him away. He was exhausted suddenly. All the walking and worry, all the disappointment, and the freezing icy wind of the mountain caught up with him like a gust of wind and left him buffeted. He was done. He was just done.

'Dad. You shouldn't have left us.'

Max wanted to scream it. To pummel it into him with shouts and fists, till he would have to hear it. But it came out broken, his voice fracturing with the feeling of it.

Dad stepped back, wary.

'I shouldn't have left you,' he said quietly, down into the snow.

'You shouldn't have put it all on me,' croaked Max.

Dad nodded slowly.

'I – I'm not good at all this, kid. I'm useless at it. I wasn't built to bring up four kids all by myself. Who is?'

Dad's voice went thick and choked at the end and Max saw his dad was crying too. His face was crumpling up and his eyes were red, and his body was trembling all over. He was shrinking away, swiping at his face with the heels of his hands, wrapping his arms round himself with shame.

'I got scared. OK? Scared and lonely and I screwed up, and I'll get it if you can't ever forgive me, mate. I will. I wouldn't blame you.'

Max wouldn't blame himself either.

Max would blame his dad, for this, forever.

But he could understand him too.

Max knew what it felt to feel like that. He was the big man, the chip off the old block, after all. Not so different. It had been hard, doing it all by himself – and not only because he was eleven. It was a hard thing to do. Dad should never have ordered him to step up. But his dad – he hadn't been given a choice either. Just cos you were the dad it didn't mean you knew how to be one.

You said yes to Nice Jackie, because you needed the money.

You ran, because staying was too hard.

You just tried to get it right, as hard as you could, and sometimes it still came out wrong.

Max thought of Bill, chopping wood, giving him time and words and the space to say them.

Max thought of Michael and Tal and the dog, together in grief.

You could learn how to be a dad, he reckoned.

If you wanted.

Max looked up at his mountain, and let himself be free of it.

# 30

He walked through the snow and held his dad, wrapping his arms tightly round him and crying with him. Needing his arms. Comforting him back.

'I love you,' he said.

He could feel his dad swallowing hard. 'Love you too, mate,' he said.

'Nice Jackie gave me a suitcase to look after.'

'Don't worry about it.'

'Dad –'

'I'll sort it out. I'm going to the police when I get back, OK? I can't keep running, can I?'

They stood in the snow, wordless.

'I'm freezing, Max,' said Dad, eventually.

'Me too.'

'Let's go in, eh?'

'Hot chocolate.'

'Good plan, big man.'

There wasn't any. There wasn't any milk left either.

'Mrs Evans has gone over to the Bevans' to shout at them,' said Thelma. 'I bet they've got hot chocolate.'

Max shook his head.

He knew they were waiting for news, perhaps bad news, the worst. Max's lies were nothing to that. They should leave them be.

But it was impossible to explain, so Max found himself standing before the Bevans' front door even more afraid than the first time.

Michael opened it, filling the space even as he stooped, huge and looming and very much alive.

'You're –' Max whispered.

The relief had no time to settle. Michael's eyes bore into Max as if he knew every inch of him. Knew about the mountain too, and Ripley on the rocks, and how stupid he'd been. Max quaked.

But Michael said nothing. He nodded and went back inside, leaving the door open for them to follow.

The living room was filled with the warm glow of the fire and the smell of oranges and cinnamon. Bill had worked a spell of some sort on Mrs Evans. She was smiling now, laughing and sipping on a glass of something red and steaming, gently stroking Tiger's nose, while Tiger, ears flat, rested her head on her knee.

'Oh, there you are,' she said. 'Bill's explained himself, a little. And apparently Max is some sort of local hero.'

'Saved a few lives, this one,' said Bill smiling. 'Called out the Mountain Rescue for some climbers, stuck in the snow.'

'Did he now?' Dad looked at Max afresh.

'I helped!' squeaked Ripley.

Max swallowed. 'Is everyone OK? It – it looked bad,' he said, looking to Michael.

Michael was leaning against the back wall, his great hairy arms folded across his broad chest. He breathed hard, nodding slowly.

'They will be, yes. Not my group. We set off early, but stayed on a short road walk. When we got back to the centre, found out some of the lads from the hostel had gone out. Mountains in that weather. They were fools to go up. Fools.'

Michael's dark eyes looked into Max.

Max swallowed. 'Wait for the weather,' he said. 'I know. I – I won't forget.'

Michael stayed quite still. But eventually he nodded, as if satisfied.

Ripley remained blessedly silent.

'The helicopter picked up two people,' Bill added, to clarify. 'Rest came down on foot. One broken leg, minor injuries, hypothermia and a bit of shock, obviously, so they've taken them in. They were lucky. Lucky it wasn't worse, lucky to have help. You're a bit of a hero, I reckon, Max.'

Max thought about clinging to the rocky scramble

with a backpack stuffed with a kitchen knife, a copper bucket and a fire blanket, in charge of a sniffly six-year-old. It hadn't felt heroic. But they'd done a good thing, calling for help. They might have saved lives.

The dog jumped up from resting on Mrs Evans's knee and scampered across the floor, tail wagging for a new arrival to the room.

Tal, lingering in the doorway.

He must have heard. He had to know how Max had been able to make the call.

Tal knelt down to fuss the dog. Stayed there, avoiding Max's eyes until Max stepped over and knelt too.

'Sorry.'

Tal nodded, his eyes on the dog.

'Could've told me you were going,' said Tal, coolly.

'I – I ran out of time. I –'

*I was scared Bill and Michael would be angry. I was scared I'd got you in trouble. I was scared you'd tell me not to be so daft, to go up in this weather.*

*And I needed to do it, now, today, and it couldn't wait.*

Max didn't know how to say any of it.

Tal kept looking at him. Then he dropped his chin.

He stroked Tiger, his voice low and tight. 'What did you find?'

'It wasn't there. Just rocks.'

Tal went quite still.

'You sure?'

He looked stricken.

Max wanted to make up a tale for him, but he was done with lies today and too tired to think.

'Sorry,' he said again, lamely.

'Right then,' said Mrs Evans, placing her glass firmly on a coaster. 'Any more of that and I'll sleep here till New Year. There's presents to wrap still. Time I was driving back.'

There was an awkward silence.

Louise looked plaintively from Max to her dad.

'Oh, for pity's sake, stop looking so miserable,' Mrs Evans said. 'I couldn't fit you all in my car anyway. And . . . well, like Bill was saying, you'll need to tidy up. Do some laundry.' She nodded at the warm fleeces, borrowed from the drawers. 'And . . . well, I think the kids deserve a bit of the Christmas holidays with their dad. Right, Pete?'

Dad nodded, swallowing thickly. 'They do, yeah.'

It seemed Bill and Mrs Evans between them had plotted it all: a not-quite-Christmas Day for the Kowalskis in the cottage, with permission this time. The Bevans were going to Llanberis that evening, visiting Michael's family. But they'd be back tomorrow, the twenty-third, and there was the mountain-centre van they could borrow to get them all home to Southend.

When Dad would go to the police.

It wasn't perfect. But it was something.

'Thanks,' said Max awkwardly, as they slowly filtered back out into the cold. It was darker now, the night drawing close.

Bill gave Max a guilty look. He dipped his head, glancing nervously at Michael as if words had already been said. 'Listen. I'm sorry, Max. I knew something wasn't right, you lot there looking after yourselves. I shouldn't have gone along with it. Should've asked the right questions, not left you to manage.'

'No need to stick your nose in, is there?' said Dad, awkward in the doorway. 'They did all right, by all accounts. Bright kids.'

Bill looked Max's dad in the eye, like he knew him of old, and he didn't much like what he knew.

'They are, very much so,' he said quietly.

'Thank you for bringing us that box of food,' said Louise. 'And teaching us how to do a fire.'

'Thanks for the Welsh cakes,' said Thelma.

'I was going to say that one!' said Ripley hotly. 'Um – thank you very much for having a nice dog.'

Bill smiled.

'I'm sorry I lied,' said Max.

'You're forgiven.'

There was a lot more Max could say. But Bill smiled, and Max felt understood, without his having to learn a new way of speaking to say it all.

# 31

It was not a usual sort of Christmas, that year.

There wasn't a tree with presents beneath it. There wasn't turkey and telly and noise as everyone tried out their new bike or speakers or toy that went bang. Santa did not arrive to fill anyone's stocking.

It wasn't even Christmas Day.

Dad had been up since four, Max guessed when he climbed from his bed. He'd put all the washing on, neatly folding anything that hadn't been used. He sent them all out for a 'Christmas walk' to the post office for milk, and when they came back the cottage was clean and warm, even the grate of the wood burner cleared of its thick coating of ashy grey. There was steaming tea on the table, in heavy mugs, and hot buttered toast, to be eaten tucked up on the sofa.

Louise went to her room, and came out looking bashful with an armful of small packages, wrapped in notepaper.

'Presents!' said Ripley, excited.

Dad coughed, an odd look on his face.

'They're only little,' said Louise, looking anxious as Ripley helped to pass them round. 'Thelma didn't think it was a good idea at all – but I really wanted to, T. I could only get things from the post office, though, so . . . well, you'll see.'

Thelma got a packet of envelopes, with flamingos drawn on them in hopeful biro.

Ripley, a roll of tape with Christmas stockings and gingerbread on it.

Max got a small bottle of Tipp-Ex, the sort you used to wipe out mistakes.

'For your trainers,' Louise explained. 'Because you liked how white they were, and they aren't any more.'

They were gone, and he didn't have the heart to tell her. But she was right: he had, and it was so kind of her to notice that he wondered how much else she saw and did not say.

'Wait. There isn't one for you,' he said.

Louise blushed. 'I bought a new notebook last week, and a pen, and . . . well, it wasn't really our money to spend anyway. So I've had mine. I'm sorry there isn't one for you either.'

She looked at Dad.

He shook his head. 'Got my present already,' he said, in a gruff voice that sounded sandy with feelings.

He pulled Ripley into his arms as if to cover them, ruffling her hair. 'Don't I, princess?'

She wriggled happily in his lap. Then she sat up crossly.

'You took down all my pictures!'

'Packed them.'

Dad nudged a bag, where the pages of charcoal angels and presents were neatly folded. 'Can't leave those behind.'

'What about the other decorations?' asked Louise.

'The Christmas stick is *not* coming home with us,' said Thelma, contemplating it warily.

It had shed some dry bark, and now looked vaguely bald in patches. In the cool of daylight, with no lights on, it was undeniably not a tree; not close to one.

'Poor stick,' said Ripley.

'I still think it's festive,' said Louise.

'I think . . .' said Dad, slowly, 'that it's a stick.'

For some reason it was funnier when he said it.

But Louise packed it anyway – carefully, in newspaper.

They did the washing-up, and wrote a note, to say sorry, and thank you, again, to Mrs Evans and Elis Evans's nain and all the rest. Everyone signed it.

They left it on the table, propped against the kettle.

'Goodbye, cottage,' called Ripley. 'Goodbye, walls, goodbye, fire, goodbye, slippers.'

'Oh god, save us,' said Thelma.

'Come *on*,' muttered Louise, clutching her notebook tightly to her chest. 'I'm in the middle of a very important chapter.'

'Someone touched someone's boob,' said Thelma. 'I read it over her shoulder.'

'You did not!' wailed Louise.

'She did, I saw,' said Ripley.

'Did she say "boob"?' asked Dad, looking nervously at Max.

Max shrugged. Not his problem.

'OK, we're definitely leaving now,' said Dad.

The slam of the cottage door felt final, and for a moment Max swayed on his feet, feeling the ache in his legs from the walk of the day before.

They weren't just going home. They were going back to face it all: everything they'd run both from. Dad knew about the suitcase, now. His lips had gone white when Max showed him. He'd gone out to the cold clear air of the garden by himself, to think. Then he'd called them all together: not just Max, but the whole family. He was going to the police when they got home, he'd told them. He'd take the suitcase; he'd tell them it was all Nice Jackie. It would help, he said. They might let him off, if he told them that.

They all knew what it meant. When he went to the police, he might not be coming back.

Now, it didn't seem such a fearful future. Perhaps they would let him off. But if Dad couldn't be with them for a bit, they still would be all right, even then. Tal had been in care. He'd come out OK. And Max didn't need a new family, like Tal had.

Asking for help: it was OK. He wouldn't mind having a bit of help.

The mountain-centre van was already open when they reached the Bevans' house. Michael sat at the wheel, too large as always.

The girls climbed in. Dad took the seat up front, beside Michael, looking vaguely terrified.

Max lingered, gazing back along the road. Back up at Y Ddraig Aur, at the zigzag path and the snow and the false peak, leading to nowhere and everywhere.

'You know, I've been thinking,' said a voice from the wall. 'About the dragon.'

Tal was sitting in a fleece and a pair of purple-and-yellow striped trousers, gazing up at the mountain too.

Max held his breath, and waited: to hear Tal say it had all been a lie. As if they'd both wanted to believe in it, and had both known it was a lie, all along.

But Tal smiled.

'They don't like the cold, dragons.'

Max nodded. Of course they didn't. It was obvious, really.

'I think,' said Tal, 'it was probably tucked up somewhere warm. Under the mountain, by the lake of gold. Till the snow melts, I think.'

Max nodded again.

'You could come back next year. We could go looking again. In spring maybe, or summer.'

'You reckon?'

Tal nodded. 'Yeah. Much better chance. They might even hibernate. Scientists don't know, do they? Summer, that's when we should go.'

And that was that.

Max felt something light settle round him, like protection. A friend, who wanted to see him again in the summer.

A plan.

Dragons to believe in.

Max climbed into the van happy, and all along the valley he watched the mountains wind away behind them, naming them under his breath like a promise: *I'll come back, I'll come back, I'll come back.*

# Acknowledgements

My heartfelt thanks to the Puffin superheroes: Ruth Knowles, who I want to be when I grow up; Emma Jones, for editorial brilliance; Stephanie Barrett and Sarah Hall; and every unnamed member of the team that brings a book to life. Special thanks to Andrew Bannecker for the incredible cover illustration and Dominica Clements for the design.

Effusive thank yous to my agent Caroline Walsh, whose positivity and support I could not do without. You believe in me when I don't, and I really appreciate it. Thanks too to Allison Cole and the rest of the team.

Love, gratitude and long-distance hugs to the Sisterhood, and the new place.

I'm indebted to the whole Gowans family for their warm hospitality and generosity. Thank you especially to Jenny, who should know by now that if she makes a casual suggestion of what I should write next, I will probably listen.

Thank you to my family for having the good sense to be Welsh, and for taking me up many mountains.

Thank you to Fliss, for all the best adventures.

Finally: much of this book was written on the 7.42 train. Thank you to my fellow commuters for politely ignoring the frantic typing woman in seat 44, and for (mostly) not eating beef-flavoured Monster Munch for breakfast.

# *A note on locations*

Y Ddraig Aur is not a real mountain's name, and there is no Welsh legend of a golden lake guarded by a dragon. Nant Glyder is not a real place, and the topography of this book is not any you will find on a map of north Wales.

Anyone familiar with Snowdonia, however, will recognise the mountain Y Ddraig Aur is based upon. The Glyders are one of the finest ranges in the National Park, and Glyder Fach's peak is rightly famous for its striking, otherworldly spiky rock structures. There is a real Castle of the Winds, and, on a day when the cloud sits low and swirls like smoke, you can very much imagine it might make a home for a dragon. (There's a real punishing scree, too.)

'Max was, he knew, doing something very stupid.' This is quite the understatement. Mountains are beautiful places to spend your time, but they deserve your respect. If Max's story inspires you to seek out a mountain or two, be like Michael: learn the right skills, take the right gear, and always wait for the weather.

Want to read more from Susie Day?
Turn the page to read an extract from

# PEA'S BOOK OF BEST FRIENDS

# CHAPTER 1

# GOODBYE

'There,' said Pea, propping up her creation on the mantelpiece. 'Told you I'd have time to finish it.'

She stepped back and considered her handiwork. It was a blue plaque – the sort they put outside houses where famous writers once lived, to make people say 'Oh!' and fall off the pavement. This one was more of a blue plate, really. The writing was in silver marker that was running out. She'd spelled *Author* wrong due to the pressure of the moment – but it would do till there was a real one.

'It's *nice*,' said Clover doubtfully, peering over

the top of Pea's head. 'But why isn't my name on it?'

'Mine isn't either,' said Pea. 'Or Tinkerbell's, though I suppose I could add us. Somewhere.'

'Don't bother with mine,' said Tinkerbell, clicking one end of a pair of handcuffs closed around her tiny wrist. '*I'm* not going anywhere.'

With a click, the other cuff snapped shut around the fat wooden leg of the sofa.

With a gulp, the key disappeared down Wuffly the dog.

It was the day the Llewellyn sisters were to leave the sleepy seaside town of Tenby for their new life in London. So far, it was not going exactly as planned. The electricity had been cut off a day too soon. Tinkerbell's father Clem (who had stayed overnight just to keep an eye on things, as he often did lately) had made a bonfire in the front yard to cook toast over, stuck on the end of a twig, and accidentally set fire to the front door. The removal van had arrived three hours early, and left without warning, taking with it breakfast, their hairbrushes, and all but one of Clover's shoes.

But not, apparently, a pair of handcuffs.

Pea was secretly pleased. Clem had put out the fire before she could dial 999, but now they had an excuse. Perhaps she could locate a kitten for the firefighters to rescue too, while they were in the area. In gratitude, they might offer to take them by fire engine all the way to London, sirens on. That would be the ideal introduction to city life.

City life was something of a mystery to Pea, but she couldn't wait to meet it. She'd made everyone play Monopoly after tea for weeks, for research. London seemed to be mostly about rent and tax, going to jail, and being a top hat. Old Kent Road was brown. According to films, there were also red buses, Victorian pickpockets, and all houses had a view of Big Ben. It was going to be brilliant.

'*Please* tell me you've got a spare key for those cuffs,' said Clem as he chased Wuffly around the ancient blue sofa.

'There's a car coming!' cried Clover, wobbling on one shoe.

Tinkerbell sat on the floorboards, cross-legged, drawing a picture of a mermaid with perfect concentration.

Wuffly made a break for the open door of the flat.

Clem gave chase.

The blue plate toppled off the mantelpiece with a smash.

Pea knelt beside the pieces, and clutched her thumbs tightly in her fists. She'd seen it on a poster in the library. It was supposed to stop you from crying – something about redirecting the electricity inside your brain. It never worked.

'Oh, don't, please don't! We can fix it!' said Clover, who hated anyone getting teary (despite being quite the expert herself), especially on important days. But the glue was in a box on its way to London. So were all the other blue plates.

'Well, we'll make another one when we

arrive. A brand-new one for our brand-new house.'

'But it isn't *for* the new house,' Pea said. The new house hadn't earned a blue plaque yet. It was for *this* house, like a goodbye present. But that was the sort of thing Clover wouldn't understand, like saving the nuttiest square of chocolate for last.

Clover eyed Tinkerbell. 'Don't stress. At this rate, we might never get there.'

Pea looked at the plate jigsaw (wondering half-heartedly if the firefighters might be able to fix it), then looked at Tinkerbell, and sighed. As the eldest, Clover was supposed to be the mean one, really, but she'd never been very good at it.

'You can't stay here, Tink,' Pea said gently, taking her drawing pencil. 'Clem burned all the chairs. And you're too little to be left behind to look after yourself.'

'I'm *seven*, not five,' said Tinkerbell drily, producing a new pencil from her pocket.

'You won't even remember this place once

you see our new house,' said Pea, watching as Tinkerbell gave the mermaid horns and a tail. 'I expect it's more like a palace, really. With turrets, a drawbridge—'

'*Loads* of handsome princes,' said Clover.

'If you like.' Pea suspected Tinkerbell would be more interested in dungeons, but Clover was thirteen, and Pea had read all about hormones and mind-altering lip gloss. She herself intended to stay sensibly eleven for as long as possible.

'She's here!' shouted Clem from the stairs as Wuffly barked a mad fanfare.

Pea ran to join Clover at the first-floor window. With a scrape, and a bit of help with pulling the sofa, Tinkerbell followed. Even Wuffly reappeared, to press her wet nose against the glass.

It was a taxi. Not the usual Tenby sort, with DAVECABS and a phone number stickered to the door, but a proper black London cab with an orange lamp. And climbing out was no ordinary passenger.

It was Mum.

Bree Llewellyn, who had lived for the last four years in this tiny first-floor flat with her three girls, making ends meet while she typed, and typed, and hoped.

But Bree Llewellyn was no more. The birdlike blonde goddess stepping out of that taxi was now better known as Marina Cove – bestselling author of the *Mermaid Girls* books.

They waited for her to wave up at them, but there was a handful of girls on the doorstep, clutching books to be signed.

'She's so good with the fans,' breathed Clover.

Privately, Pea thought Clover sounded a bit daft when she repeated other grown-ups' words like that. But it was true: their mother always gave her readers plenty of attention. They watched her pose for photographs, and write her not-real name in the front of books, and Pea very quietly and privately missed the days when she had belonged just to them. Tinkerbell's mermaid, with the horns and tail, ended up on top of a thickly scribbled furniture bonfire, engulfed in red-pencil flames.

Then there were footsteps on the stairs, dainty and clicky.

There she was in the open doorway, great clouds of blonde hair flowing over her shoulders, long skirt shimmering like silver scales. Marina Cove, the famous writer.

'What *have* you done to our front door?' she said, folding her arms severely across her chest.

And then she was Mum again, and everything was all right.

Pea showed her the bits of blue plate, and felt herself wrapped up in a hug that seemed to put it back together again – all wool and hair, and the perfume-smell of jasmine flowers.

Clover limped over – the one shoe that had been left behind was a clog – and joined in, while Clem explained about the fire, and the chairs, and why no one had brushed their hair. (Not that anyone would've noticed. Clover resembled her mother exactly, including the ability to roll out of bed with hair all twirled and tousled as if it had been arranged that way on purpose. Tinkerbell took after her father, Clem, who was Jamaican by way of Birmingham, so her curls needed rebraiding tightly to her head once a week with a blob of CurlyGurl coconut goop to stop her from going fluffy. Only Pea required a regular morning taming, but on Clover's advice she was learning to describe her bright orange mane as 'Pre-Raphaelite' as opposed to 'ginger frizz'. In any case, it did the job of distracting from her chin, which was of a size people mention.)

'I did try,' said Clem, who was looking quite tired by now, and kept glancing hopefully at his watch.

'Oh, who cares about a few tangles,' said Mum. 'I've been looking forward to today for so long, my darlings, and I'm not going to let a single thing ruin it.'

Pea winced, and reluctantly stepped back so Mum could see Tinkerbell.

But Tinkerbell was sitting on the sofa, quite unhandcuffed, throwing a scrumpled ball of drawing paper for Wuffly to chase.

'There you are, pickle!' said Mum, sweeping her up into a great whirling hug of her own. 'Have you been awful for Daddy? I hope so.'

'Of course I had a spare key,' Tinkerbell hissed, once Mum had let her go and gone off to inspect the oddly naked kitchen. She dropped the key into Clem's hands, reluctantly followed by the cuffs. 'You won't tell, will you?'

Clem shook his head wearily.

It was time to go. Especially for Clem, whose job was showing empty houses to people like Mum who needed new ones, and who was supposed to have been unlocking 8 Harbour Court for a nice young couple from Saundersfoot an hour ago.

'See you soon then, girls,' he said, kissing

Mum's cheek. 'I'll come up to visit, check out your new digs once you're all settled, right?'

*Marina lives with her three girls and a dog by the sea* – that's what it said on the back page of the *Mermaid Girls* books. Clem hadn't lived with them for three years, and he was technically only Tinkerbell's dad. But he was still Pea's Clem – and Clover's, and always a little bit Mum's. Suddenly it felt quite wrong to be going off to all the exciting tax and jail and pickpockets without him.

'Weekly email with all your news, remember?' he whispered in Pea's ear when it was her turn for a goodbye hug.

'With bullet points,' she whispered back, holding on extra tight.

He thudded down the stairs at speed.

'Will he really come to visit?' asked Tinkerbell.

'Of course! We're moving to London, not Mars,' said Mum, tucking Tinkerbell's chin into the crook of her arm. 'Now come on, before that taxi driver thinks we've changed our minds.'

She hurried them out with their one remaining suitcase before anyone could stop for a last look and feel the tiniest bit sad.

'Goodbye, little flat!' she shouted as she tapped down the stairs.

'Goodbye, shower that never stays hot!' sang Clover.

'Goodbye, mouldy ceiling!' said Pea.

'Goodbye, home,' said Tinkerbell.

And they all piled into the black cab. There was a NO DOGS sign, but the driver (whose name was Alexei, and who greeted them all by name like beloveds) said, 'Don't you worry about that, kitten,' to Mum with a wink, and waited for Wuffly to pile in too.

It had nothing to do with fame, Pea knew; people had always liked doing things for their mum. They got a glazed look in their eyes, and suddenly volunteered to carry her luggage, or let her live on their houseboat in Norway for four months. Clover called it being *Mummified*, and was showing every sign of having inherited the talent. Pea was still waiting for hers to develop.

The taxi was much bigger than an ordinary car, and there were flip-down seats opposite the usual kind, which meant you went backwards. Pea and Tinkerbell bagsied them at once, though they promised to swap on the English side of the Severn Bridge if the others wanted a turn. There was also an enormous wicker hamper taking up most of the space in between.

'Who's hungry?' said Mum, flipping open the lid. There were little cakes, miniature bagels stuffed with smoked salmon and cream cheese and small sprigs of something green and grasslike, and real china plates, buckled neatly into place.

Clover and Tinkerbell sat on their hands. Pea was re-reading *A Little Princess*, and they knew perfectly well that she'd spent half the morning making cheese and onion sandwiches to finish up the leftover bread, just in case they suddenly became poor again on the way to London.

But Pea tucked the clingfilmed parcels out of sight, and helped herself without a word.

The others followed suit.

Alexei had two chocolate éclairs, posted through the money-slot of his hatch.

The journey was long. They made a list of all the London places they would visit: the Tower, the Eye, the tea rooms at the V&A (which, Mum promised, had a mad ceiling and very large cakes). Pea read more of her book. Mum gave Clover a pattern book, with real swatches of fabric and rectangles of wallpaper, for her to pick out what she'd like in her new bedroom. Mum discovered the cheese and onion sandwiches, which she said had been a very sensible idea of Pea's, and ate one to prove it. Tinkerbell fed the rest to Wuffly, until she started making peculiar doggy coughs, and had to have a lie down and a belly-rub.

The motorway turned into a busy ring road, then crowded streets lined with unfamiliar shops:

Food & Wine and Chicken Cottage. It didn't look anything like the Monopoly board.

The taxi swung into a quieter road, past a big green park, and puttered to a halt.

Mum said this was north-west London – Kensal Rise (though Alexei had said they should tell everyone it was Queen's Park, as it sounded 'more nobby').

'So, darlings, do you think I picked us a nice one?' She pointed at the house before them, half hidden by a tree: pebbly walls, a crazy-paving path and a red-brick gatepost.

'It's . . . It's . . . Is it really all ours?' said Clover breathlessly.

'Well, only this side,' said Mum quickly, before Clover could mentally annex next door for her own personal music room. 'It's semi-detached. But yes, this whole half is all ours.'

Pea watched Clover anxiously, for she'd been the most excited of them all, and a whole half was still a half, when it came down to it. But Clover began counting off windows – two on the ground floor, two more on the next, and that was just at the front – and she almost skipped up to the front door, leaving her one clog abandoned on the crazy paving behind her.

Tinkerbell regarded the house with suspicion. Wuffly gave another strange cough, then deposited a small puddle of sick on the pavement.

'Good dog,' said Tinkerbell by way of agreement, then shooed her up the path after Clover.

There weren't any turrets, or a drawbridge, Pea noted. Not much chance of a dungeon. But there was a tiny slanted window set into the roof.

'That's an attic, up there,' said Mum, as if she were looking at the house from inside Pea's head. 'It's a bit poky, but I thought you might like it for your bedroom. If you wanted.'

A bedroom, all to herself. In an attic, where she could pretend to be impoverished if being famous and wealthy got a bit dull. She could write her own books up there. One day, perhaps, there would be a blue plaque on the wall outside for Pea Llewellyn, famous writer.

Pea stepped over the sick, and the clog, and ran up the path.

Flat 2B,
Painter Drive, Tenby
Here lived
MARINA COVE
(also known as Bree Llewellyn)
Autpr

# Have you read them all?

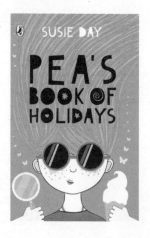

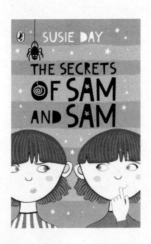

susieday.com

@mssusieday